I0534846

A WITCH FOR MR. BELL

WITCHES OF CHRISTMAS GROVE
BOOK SEVEN

DEANNA CHASE

Copyright © 2025 by Deanna Chase

Editing: Angie Ramey

Cover image: © Ravven

ISBN 978-1-965804-14-8

All rights reserved. No part of this publication may be reproduced, stored in, or introduced into a retrieval system, or transmitted in any form, or by any means (electronic, mechanical, photocopying, recording, or otherwise) without the prior written permission of both the copyright owner and the publisher of this book.

This book is a work of fiction. Names, characters, places, and incidents are products of the author's imagination or are used fictitiously. Any resemblance to actual events, locals, business establishments, or persons, living or dead, are entirely coincidental.

Bayou Moon Press, LLC

www.deannachase.com

Printed in the United States of America

ABOUT THIS BOOK

Earth witch Felicity Hill is fiercely independent and isn't interested in romance. She likes a fun date, but when it comes to commitment, forget it. Her parents' broken marriage ruined that for her when she was just a kid. But what she is interested in, is saving her family land from being sold to the highest bidder. And this Christmas she'll do whatever it takes to make sure that no part of the original Hill family property is turned into high density condos... even if it means working with the one man who makes her want things she shouldn't.

Jackson Bell used to be a high-powered businessman. But these days, he's only interested in the slower paced lifestyle he's found in the enchanted small town of Christmas Grove... and the feisty woman, Felicity Hill, who owns the Apples and Spice and Everything Nice farm.

CHAPTER 1

"*I* really wish you'd hire someone else to fix those Christmas lights," Marilyn said as she stopped her truck next to the large fir tree that was right at the entrance to Felicity's property. The acreage was home to her apple orchard, Apples and Spice and Everything Nice, a specialty store, and a cozy cabin that she rented out to tourists. One of the strands of lights had suddenly stopped working, and someone needed to climb up the ladder to fix it.

Felicity Hill frowned at her office manager, who'd been her late grandmother's best friend, and said, "You know as well as I do that we can't afford that. We're barely making enough to keep this place running as it is."

"I'd rather take a pay cut than see you climbing a ladder, Felicity Rose. Especially in this weather."

"You did not just middle name me," Felicity said with a smile at her favorite person in the world.

"You're darn right I did," she said, her piercing green eyes boring a hole in Felicity's head. "And I'll do it again and again and again when you're being stubborn."

"I'm not being stubborn," Felicity insisted. "I'm being frugal. There's a difference. And what are you talking about with the weather? It's cold, but that's all. It'll take me like five minutes to fix those lights."

"Fine. Then I'm waiting here until you're done," Marilyn said.

"You can't," Felicity said with a sigh. "You have just enough time to get to the bank before they close." She hopped out and held the truck door open as she added, "Go make that deposit so the checks to our vendors don't bounce. I promise to be careful."

Marilyn scowled. "If I find you buried in the snow in the morning, I'm going to whip your hide. Understand?"

Felicity raised her hand and saluted her friend. "Yes, ma'am."

"Sass. You have too much of it."

"Just the right amount." Felicity shut the door, hauled the ladder out of the truck bed, and then waved as Marilyn took off.

Felicity set up the ladder next to the tree, checked to be sure it was secure, and then clasped her hands together and blew on her frozen fingers. Why did the string of Christmas lights that went out have to be on the tallest tree on her property? The tree that was the first one all her customers saw when they drove into the entrance of Apples and Spice and Everything Nice.

Marilyn was right. She should have hired Randy the handyman. But then she'd have to put something else off, like getting the HVAC serviced. She sighed to herself. There was barely enough money to pay her two shop workers this season, let alone anyone else. If she wanted the lights to work on the large fir tree, it was up to her to fix them.

The rumble of a truck sounded behind her, and when she turned, she spotted a familiar Ford F150 turning into her lane. A tiny smile tugged at her lips when the truck came to an idle next to her. "Well, hello there, Jackson Bell. You're a little late, aren't you?"

"It's been a busy day," he said, his gaze scanning her body like a wolf eyeing his next prey.

"Stop it," she said with a smirk.

"Stop what?" His easy smile reached his beautiful dark eyes. Damn he was gorgeous. It was too bad he was the commitment type. Because otherwise, she'd be all in on that hot fling they'd started and stopped a month ago.

"Undressing me with your eyes," she said. "Go on up to the store. Your crates of apples are on the porch."

"What about you? Do you need a ride up the hill?" he asked.

"No, thanks. I'm good." She waved him off. "Go before you're late for work. I'd hate for the patrons of Sleighed to have to wait for their burrata sandwiches and truffle fries."

"No one will have to wait," he said. "Everything is already prepped." Jackson was the cook at her bestie's pub, and honestly, his food was some of her favorite in all of Christmas Grove.

"Okay, Mr. Prepared. Go get your apples, and maybe I'll come by the pub for some apple pie later."

"I'm counting on it." He winked and then took off up the hill.

Felicity waited until the truck was out of sight before she turned to the ladder and sighed. After checking to be sure it was stable, Felicity climbed up carefully, one rung at a time. She was careful not to look down, as that was a surefire way to cause her to get dizzy. The last thing on her to-do list was to pass out and fall to her death. Just because she wasn't a fan of Christmas, that didn't mean she wanted to check out altogether. She did love her little farm and her friends. And the town of Christmas Grove. It was just that the month of December hadn't always been kind to her, and every year when Christmas rolled around, she was reminded of a past she'd sooner forget.

Still, her customers loved Christmas, so it was up to her to fix the twinkling lights.

"Okay, lights. Work with me here," she said as she tested each bulb, pulling them out and trying a new one. It wasn't until she got down to the second to last one that her new bulb did the trick. As soon as she shoved it into the socket, the lights lit and started twinkling in the gray light. She grinned, pleased with a job well done, and then started to climb back down.

Just as she reached the bottom rung and was about to hop off the ladder, Felicity heard the rumble of Jackson's truck coming down the hill. She briefly wondered what had taken him so long to grab his apples, but then suddenly a Jeep turned onto her road, barreling straight at the truck.

Felicity's life flashed before her eyes as Jackson swerved toward her. The sound of a shrill horn filled the air as the truck hit the snow bank just to her left, causing the ladder to topple over. She crashed into a mound of fresh powdery snow and let out an *oomph* as the wind was knocked out of her.

Blinking up at the rapidly darkening sky, Felicity took stock of her body. Her frozen toes still worked, and the ice-cold sting of the snow on her back indicated that she wasn't in fact paralyzed by the fall. If wiping out in a pile of snow wasn't bad enough, she suddenly realized she'd done it right in front of Jackson Bell.

Great.

The door of the truck slammed and was quickly followed by Jackson peering over her. "Felicity? Are you okay?"

"I think so," she said as snow started to fall from the rapidly darkening sky. "How's your truck?"

He glanced at his vehicle before ignoring the question and reaching down to take her hand in his. "Let me help you up."

She tightened her grip and dug in her heels as he hauled her to her feet. Loose snow flew from her clothes, and when the wind picked up, her entire body shivered. Her soaking wet sweater clung to her skin, making her teeth chatter. She had no choice but to pull it off, leaving her in only a white tank top and her wet jeans.

"Nice top." He stared right at her chest and then looked up at her with the wolfish grin again.

Felicity glanced down at herself and realized she looked like she was a contestant in a wet T-shirt contest. She quickly clasped her arms over her chest, remembering too late that she'd opted to go braless after the underwire broke through and started poking her in the chest. "Sweet baby Rudolph," she muttered. "Could this day get any worse?"

"Funny, I was just thinking it was getting better," he teased and then pulled his own sweater off and handed it to her. "Take this until we can find you something else to wear."

He was wearing a skintight T-shirt that didn't leave anything to the imagination, and her gaze landed on that well-defined chest that had haunted her dreams ever since she'd succumbed to his charms and spent the night with him a month ago.

"Felicity? Need help putting that on?" Jackson asked, his smile widening.

"No," she said, snapping out of her lust haze as she tugged on the sweater. "Thank you. That was very kind. But now you must be freezing."

"I'll survive until I get into the truck. Come on. Let's put that ladder in the back and I'll drive you up to the store."

"You don't need to do that," Felicity said. "Marilyn and I can get it in the morning."

He glanced over to where the ladder had fallen. "Do you really think you two will be able to find it after it snows all night?"

She followed his gaze and grimaced. The snow had started to come down at a steady pace. It would be buried in no time. "You have a point. Okay. Let's get it in the back of the truck."

Jackson walked over to the ladder, hauled it out of the snow, and threw it in the back of his truck before she even managed to walk the few feet to the vehicle.

"Impressive," she said, wondering exactly how many hours the man spent in the gym each day. His muscles were rippling through the T-shirt, making her face flush with heat despite the cold.

He chuckled softly and opened the passenger door for her. "Come on. Let's get you somewhere warm."

She gladly climbed into the passenger seat, grateful he was there to help. Once he was back in the driver's seat, she asked, "Did you see where that Jeep went?"

"Up the hill." He put the truck in gear and thankfully was able to back out of the snowbank without any trouble.

"What are they still doing up there?" she asked out loud. "The store is closed. Unless they are the short-term-rental guests." She groaned, realizing that was probably the case. "Hopefully they didn't run over anything else."

"They were probably just distracted, trying to make sure they were in the right place," Jackson said, being far too charitable.

"Or they are entitled a-holes who don't care about anyone else. They didn't even stop to be sure we were both okay," she said, wondering if she should ask them to leave rather than let them stay in her cabin. They could have gotten her killed with their reckless driving.

"Always possible," Jackson said as he parked the truck next to the black Jeep that was idling in front of the store.

Felicity jumped out and ran over to the Jeep, ready to give the driver a piece of her mind.

A man who looked to be in his early fifties climbed out of the Jeep, and before she could say anything, he held out a manila envelope. "Felicity Hill?"

"Yes, I'm Felicity, and you are?" she asked as she took the envelope.

"You've been served." He got back in his Jeep and took off down the hill.

Felicity stared at the envelope, shellshocked. "Served? For what?"

"You're going to have to open it to find out," Jackson said.

She jerked her head up, realizing that he was standing in front of her, freezing in his T-shirt. "Here," she said, pulling his sweater off and handing it to him. "Go on. I'm sure this is nothing. You need to get to work."

Jackson frowned. "Are you sure? I could—"

"I'm sure," she said quickly, the cold seeping into her bones. "I'm just going to go inside, get a hot cup of coffee, and then deal with this after my fingers defrost. I'll come by Sleighed after I stop by my house and get changed."

"If you're sure," he said, obviously hesitating.

She pasted on a smile. "I'm sure. Go on. I'll see you later."

Jackson waited a beat but then nodded. "Tonight. I'm counting on it."

Felicity pulled out her keys, unlocked the store that she'd locked up before Marilyn took her down the hill, and then walked in, grateful for the warmth. She walked into the office, tossed the envelope onto her desk, and then peeled her T-shirt off before pulling on a cozy hoodie. She immediately felt better, despite her still-wet jeans.

After grabbing a cup of coffee, she pulled the paperwork from the envelope.

Loan overdue was stamped on the top of the first page. "What loan?" she asked no one as she scanned the document. There was a modest amount listed as the original loan with a date from over fifty years ago. It was a simple agreement that the loan would be paid off by Dec 31, 2025. Below that was an enormous amount of interest, making the eye-popping amount due completely unattainable. The second page was a signed contract with what looked to be her grandmother's signature. She squinted at the bubbly cursive and frowned. Her grandmother's signature was messier than that, wasn't it?

Felicity scoffed, assuming it was some sort of scam. She wasn't an idiot and certainly wouldn't be falling for something so blatant. She shoved the paper back into the envelope and made a mental note to call her lawyer about it in the morning before she tossed it out.

A loud knock on the door startled her out of her thoughts. She grabbed her cup of coffee and went to the door, assuming it was her short-term renters, and grateful she'd be able to go home soon.

But instead of the couple she was expecting, Jackson stood on the porch, his hands shoved in his pockets. The snow was really coming down now, and she decided she should get on the road soon if she didn't want to get snowed in. "Hey," she said as she opened the door for him. "Did you forget something?"

"No," he said, shaking his head. "The road just before the bridge is closed due to a fallen tree, so I can't get out."

"We can't get over the bridge?" she asked, shocked. "You're sure?"

He chuckled softly. "Would I be here if I wasn't? You're not going to make me spend the night in my truck, are you?"

"No, of course not." She opened the door, inviting him in. And as she closed it again, she turned and asked, "Night? You think it's going to be closed until morning?"

"At least. The storm is here. No one is clearing trees until the snow stops," he said.

Her phone buzzed with a message. It was from her short-term renters. The highway was closed due to snow. They weren't coming.

She looked up at Jackson. "Looks like we just lucked out."

"How's that?"

"The cabin just opened up," she said.

"You're inviting me to spend the night with you in the cabin?" he asked, seemingly surprised.

"I guess you could stay in the office if you want, but I'm going where there's a fireplace and groceries stocked. Your choice."

"The cabin it is," he said, following her toward the door.

Felicity grabbed the keys to the cabin, swallowed hard, and wondered exactly how she was going to keep her hands off the incredibly irresistible Jackson Bell.

CHAPTER 2

*J*ackson gritted his teeth against the chill as he climbed out of his truck. He'd followed Felicity's Jeep a quarter mile down the road to the secluded cabin, grateful for the heater in his truck. The temps had dropped and the wind was whipping through his sweater.

"Your teeth are chattering," she said as she unlocked the cabin door.

"I'll be fine once we get inside," he said.

"Not until we get the fire started," she said.

"No central heat. Great."

Felicity chuckled. "It's a cabin retreat, meant to be cozy. Don't worry. There are blankets and a hot shower. You won't freeze."

He definitely wouldn't. Just being near Felicity got him heated.

She'd been spot on about needing that fire. The cabin

was an icebox when they first walked in. Jackson wasted zero time getting the fire started. Thankfully, there was a Firestarter log ready to go in the fireplace as well as a metal container of chopped wood to keep it going through the night. While Felicity disappeared into the small kitchen, Jackson got the fire to a dull roar, and when she returned with two cups of hot cocoa, his teeth had finally stopped chattering.

"Excellent job, boy scout," she said, handing him the cocoa.

"I'd say thank you, but that Firestarter log was a cheat." He wrapped his hand around the mug and grinned at her. "Brilliant, but a cheat."

"Gotta make it pleasant for the guests," she said. Her phone buzzed and she quickly answered it, assuring the other person on the line that she was fine and safe for the night.

Jackson pulled out his phone and called Marissa.

She answered on the first ring. "Jackson. Please tell me you're not stranded in a ditch somewhere in this weather."

"I'm not in a ditch, but I am stranded at Apples and Spice and Everything Nice. After I picked up the apples, a tree fell and we can't get out. It looks like we're gonna be here for the night."

"We?" she asked.

"Yeah, me and Felicity. Her renters had to cancel, so we're holed up in the cabin."

There was silence for a moment, and then Marissa

cleared her throat. Amusement was clear in her tone when she said, "That's a lucky break, isn't it?"

"Yes," he said. "I'm not complaining."

She laughed. "I bet you aren't. Don't worry about things here. I'm closing up early, and Danny's taking me home before the roads are completely impassable." There was more than a little innuendo in her voice when she added, "Have a good night."

"I'll try." He ended the call and wondered if Marissa knew that he'd spent that one night with Felicity. He certainly hadn't told her. He wasn't the kiss and tell type. But she was best friends with Felicity, so it was possible *she'd* told Marissa. But, maybe not. Jackson hadn't exactly been shy about his interest in the woman sitting next to him.

Once Jackson ended his call, he sat on the sofa and took a sip of his cocoa.

Felicity was standing near the fireplace, soaking in the warmth. When she turned around, she said, "That was Clara, wondering if I was caught in a snowdrift."

"Did she make it home all right?" Clara was Felicity's other best friend, and she owned a glassblowing shop in downtown Christmas Grove.

"Yes. Is Marissa still at Sleighed?"

Jackson nodded. "She's closing early and Danny's taking her home."

"Good," Felicity said with a sigh of relief. "I also got a text from Marilyn that she made it to the bank on time and is currently tucked in her house as well."

"Sounds like everyone is in good shape to weather the storm," he said. "Thanks for putting me up by the way."

She shook her head at him. "There's no need to thank me. You'd do the same."

"True." He glanced at the kitchen. "Is there food in there? Enough to make something for dinner?"

"Yes. Part of the service is stocking the cabin so that guests don't have to run out for groceries. Once I finish this cocoa, I'll go in and make something," she said as she closed her eyes, looking exhausted.

"No way. Let me do that." Jackson rose and was already in the kitchen when he heard her mutter something. "What was that?"

"I said thank goodness," she said as she appeared in the doorway. "I can boil water and scramble some eggs, but that's about the extent of my culinary prowess."

Jackson pulled out a box of tomato basil pasta and said, "Lucky for you, you're snowed in with a chef."

"Very lucky." She looked down at her still-wet jeans and said, "If you're good here, I think I'm going to go get cleaned up."

"Go ahead. Dinner will be ready in about thirty minutes," he said as he grabbed a jar of sun-dried tomatoes from the cabinet.

With her cocoa in hand, Felicity disappeared.

Jackson found a bottle of wine, opened it to let it breathe, and then made the pasta, marveling at how well she'd stocked the kitchen for her guests.

By the time Felicity returned, he had two plates of

chicken and sun-dried tomato basil pasta on the table along with a loaf of fresh rosemary ciabatta bread.

"It smells wonderful in here," Felicity said.

"Thank you." When Jackson looked up from the table, his mouth began to water, and it had nothing to do with the pasta. Felicity was standing across from him in a fluffy terrycloth robe, her skin pink from the shower and her thick blond hair tied up in a haphazard bun. All he wanted to do was haul her off to the bedroom and devour every inch of her.

"Jackson?" she asked, looking amused.

"Yeah?"

"Is dinner ready?" She waved at the table. "Want me to pour the wine?"

"No. I mean yes," he stammered, feeling like an idiotic fifteen-year-old. "Dinner is ready, but I've got the wine. Go ahead and take a seat."

She sat at the small two-person table while Jackson poured the wine.

Once he was seated, he held his glass up and said, "To good company, a hot meal, and a warm place to ride out the storm."

"I'll toast to that," Felicity said as she clinked her glass to his.

Jackson took a sip of wine as he watched Felicity take a bite of the pasta.

"Oh wow, Jackson." She closed her eyes and let out a tiny moan of pleasure before she said, "This is delicious."

She was going to kill him. How was he going to survive the night alone with her if she kept making those noises?

"You should start serving this at Sleighed." She grinned at him and took a long sip of the wine.

"Maybe I will." He certainly would if it meant she'd spend more time there. He didn't know why he was so drawn to Felicity. Sure, she was gorgeous and fun to be around, but she'd already told him she wasn't looking for a long-term relationship. But he was. He'd always known he wanted a life partner. He just hadn't found the right woman yet.

Or at least he hadn't until he met Felicity.

Too bad she was only interested in having a little fun.

"So, what should we do to pass the time tonight, Felicity?" Jackson asked just as she was biting into a piece of bread. "Any ideas?"

She choked.

Jackson couldn't help chuckling. "Oh, I see."

"Stop," she said, laughing. "I just swallowed wrong."

"That's what she said."

Felicity rolled her eyes. "There are some games in the chest in the living room. Cards, too. Also some movies on DVD. We'll find something wholesome to do."

"Wholesome, right." He winked at her and drank some more wine.

"Get your mind out of the gutter." She stood and cleared their empty plates. "I'll clean in here. You go pick a game or movie or get a shower if you like. There's plenty of hot water. I'll meet you in the living room when I'm done."

Jackson hesitated for a few beats and then left the kitchen. He briefly contemplated a shower but decided against it for the moment. Both of them wrapped up in robes was a disaster waiting to happen. Instead, he checked out the chest in the living room. When he didn't find a game that interested him, he looked in the closet and grinned when he spotted the perfect activity.

Once he pulled the boxes out of the closet, he synced his phone to the speaker that was on the mantel and chose a Christmas music station.

By the time Felicity made her way into the living room, he had the fake Christmas tree put together and set in the window just waiting for them to decorate it.

She stopped mid-step, staring first at the tree and then at Jackson.

"Surprise!" he said, holding up a delicate glass apple ornament. "I can't think of anything better to do on a stormy night like tonight than decorate this tree."

Anger flashed in her bright blue eyes as she stalked over to him, grabbed the ornament from his hand, and carefully put it back in the box. Then without a word, she disappeared into the bedroom and slammed the door.

Jackson stared after her, shocked by her reaction. Then his heart sank as he realized he'd majorly overstepped. Feeling awful, he turned off the music and got to work taking the tree down and putting everything back where he found it.

CHAPTER 3

Felicity stood in the bedroom of the cabin and sucked in a deep breath. She needed to go back out there and apologize. Or at least explain herself. She felt like a major fool, getting so upset about the tree, but the apples... They'd brought everything back from that night six years ago.

The anger. The pain. The heartbreak.

It had been six years, and she still wasn't able to face those apples.

"Get it together, Felicity," she told herself. "You're going to have to face him at some point." It wasn't like she could just lock herself in the bedroom and expect him to sleep on the couch without any blankets or a pillow. One way or another, she'd have to leave the bedroom.

Feeling like a fool, she tentatively pulled the door open to find Jackson taking the Christmas tree down. She glanced at the window, noting the snow clinging to the glass, and then she eyed the flames flickering in the fireplace.

Cozy. That was the only way to describe the scene.

And she'd ruined it.

"Jackson, wait," she said.

He straightened and turned around to face her. "Wait for what?"

"Don't put the tree away," she said as she walked over to him and took the section of tree he'd just removed and put it back on the metal pole. "I overreacted. Majorly. Setting up the tree would make the cabin more festive. I'm sure my next guests would quite enjoy it."

"But you won't," he said, already reaching for the section of tree she'd just replaced.

"It's not the tree," she said quickly. "It's the apples." Her voice cracked on the word *apples*, and she had to turn away so he wouldn't see the tears shining in her eyes.

"I see," he said softly. "I've already put those away, so if you want to decorate this tree, I'm here to serve in any way you wish."

She turned back to him, her lips twitching into the tiniest hint of a smile. "Why does that sound dirty?"

"Because your mind is in the gutter," he said. "Just where I like it."

She laughed, feeling a weight lift off her shoulders. Jackson always had a way of making her feel lighter. How did he do that?

"Now, tell me which ornaments you want to use, and I'll unpack them while you place them on the tree," he said.

"Anything but the apples," she said, her smile fading a bit. But in an effort to keep the mood light, she pushed those memories to the back of her mind and tried to focus on the Christmases she'd spent with her two best friends, Marissa and Clara, instead. The ones when they wore onesie pajamas, spiked their hot chocolates with Irish Cream, and watched Hallmark movies until all hours of the night while making fun of the silly plotlines that they all secretly loved.

"Is that a smile I see?" Jackson asked as he opened a box of handblown glass ornaments that had been purchased from Clara's shop.

"I was just wishing that the cabin had a television so that I could force you to watch Hallmark movies while we decorate this tree."

"Is that right?" His eyes sparkled with amusement. "I've got a laptop. Does this joint have internet?"

"It does!" She laughed. "You're really game for watching cheesy Christmas movies?"

"Bring it on, Felicity," he said as he reached for the backpack he'd brought in with him. A moment later, he had the laptop open and asked for the password.

"ApplePie1942." She typed it in for him and waited. And waited some more.

They tried again before concluding that the internet must be out due to the storm.

"Darn it!" Felicity said. "I think there was a good one on tonight, too. *Sleighed Inn.*" She cackled and added, "I'm pretty sure it's about a couple that get snowed in at a remote inn in the woods."

Jackson laughed. "You mean we're a cliché already?"

"Looks like it." Felicity nudged him playfully, nearly sending them both to the hardwood floor.

"Whoa," he said softly as he grabbed her around the waist and stabilized them both. "Careful. We don't want to break anything."

"Right. Cleaning up those ornaments would be a pain," she said.

"I meant bones, but that's true, too," he said.

There was an awkward silence as they stood together with Jackson's arms around Felicity. He cleared his throat and then let her go as he took a step back, much to her disappointment. As far as she was concerned, he could have held her all night. Just as long as it was *only* for the night.

"If we can't have Christmas movies, how about a little music?" Jackson said and tapped his phone to start the music station again. "Grandma Got Run Over by a Reindeer" came on, making them both laugh.

"Perfect," Felicity said, grinning at him. She didn't know how it was possible, but Jackson Bell was turning out to be just as much fun, if not more, than her two besties. And for the first time all night, she finally admitted to herself that she was actually happy to be snowed in with him.

With the Christmas music filling the cabin and the tree coming to life, Felicity found herself sneaking glances at Jackson. He had a natural ease about him that somehow settled her. For six years, she'd felt like she'd been operating on pure nerves each Christmas season. It was both a month that she just wanted to curl up and pretend it didn't exist,

and one where she had to be at the top of her game since it was the busiest time of year at Apples and Spice and Everything Nice.

Christmas Grove always thrived during the season, since there were so many tourists who frequented the magical holiday town. It meant all the businesses were busier than ever, making the majority of their income between Thanksgiving and New Year's Day. So every year, she pasted on a smile, and during operating hours, pretended that she was just as jolly as everyone else.

But in reality, she just couldn't wait until the season was over.

"Everything okay?" Jackson asked her.

"Huh?" She looked up from the ornament she had in her hand.

"You look a little... distracted," he said, taking the ornament and placing it on the tree.

That was a nice way of putting it. If she had to guess, she probably seemed glum, but he was too polite to say so. "I was just counting the days until the holidays are over."

He raised one eyebrow. "You live in Christmas Grove and don't like the holidays?"

"Blasphemy, right?" she said, forcing a smile as she took a seat on the couch. "I didn't always feel this way."

He took a seat next to her. "What happened?"

Felicity stared at the fire. "Six years ago, we lost my grandmother right before Christmas. It was unexpected, and ever since then..." She shrugged. "It's hard to get through."

Sympathy shone in his dark eyes. "That makes sense. Are the apples hers?"

A lump formed in Felicity's throat. "Yes. She made them herself."

Jackson scooted over and slipped an arm around her shoulders, pulling her in close.

She leaned her head on his shoulder, wondering what had possessed her to open up to him. She never talked about her grandma. Not to anyone she dated, anyway.

Not that she was dating Jackson.

"I'm sorry. It sounds like she was very special," he said softly.

"She was." Felicity sucked in a halting breath and then let out a humorless laugh. She couldn't believe she was on the verge of blubbering in Jackson's arms. All over a box of glass apples. "I think I'm going to need some more wine."

"I can make that happen." He rose, disappeared into the kitchen, and a few moments later, reappeared with two glasses and a bottle of wine. "Here."

She held both glasses while he filled them with merlot.

Once he was settled beside her, he said, "I was really close to my great-aunt when I was a kid. She was the main reason I started skiing competitively."

"Really?" Felicity knew he'd been a competitive skier at one point, but she didn't know when he'd stopped or why. "Did she tear up the slopes with you or something?"

Jackson threw his head back and laughed. "Tilly on skis? No. I'm not sure she ever participated in any sport her entire life."

"Okay. Then how did she influence you to enter the world of competitive sports?" Felicity took a long sip of her wine, grateful to be talking about someone other than her grandmother.

"She lived with us after my mother left," he said. "My dad worked all the time, which is likely why she abandoned us." Jackson let out a sad, humorless laugh. "Tilly was the person who was there for me. No matter what I was interested in, she always encouraged me to go after it. She'd say, 'Jackson, don't let anyone tell you you're not good enough. If you want to ski, then you should ski. Fall on your face and get back up and do it all over again and again and again. If you're passionate about it, then embrace it. Love it. Put your heart into it.'"

"Tilly sounds wonderful," Felicity said. "And your dad? Was he encouraging?"

Jackson shrugged. "I suppose? But only when he realized I was good enough to be a contender for the US team. Prior to that he really didn't say much. Especially since Tilly always told him to get on board or keep his thoughts to himself." There was a light in Jackson's eye now and a genuine smile. "She was the only person on earth who could put him in his place."

"And your mom? Did you see her after she left?" Felicity asked. His smile faded, and she instantly regretted her question. "I'm sorry. You don't have to answer that. It's none of my business." Her own mother had left Christmas Grove when Felicity was just fifteen. After her parents' divorce, Rebecca had decided she needed a fresh start somewhere else. When Felicity had refused to leave, she'd left her with her grandmother.

"It's fine," Jackson said, his voice flat. "Our relationship is complicated. She moved out of state and I only saw her a couple of times when I was a kid. A few years ago, she decided she wanted to reconnect, but it's been rocky at best. She came here for the Christmas season that year, but I haven't seen her since."

"I bet Tilly has some choice words for her," Felicity said.

"She used to. My aunt passed a few years before my dad did."

The sadness in his expression made Felicity reach out and squeeze his hand. What she really wanted to do was wrap her arms around him and... do what? Reassure him that he wasn't alone? From the woman who wasn't interested in a long-term relationship? Those words would seem awfully empty coming from her. She had her friends to call family. She assumed he did, too. He was close to Danny and Marissa, but otherwise, she really didn't know who he called family.

"I think we need more wine," she said.

He nodded. "I couldn't agree more."

CHAPTER 4

"*I* think I has... um *had* too much wine," Felicity said, slurring her words a little. She hiccuped and then let out a small giggle.

"You're probably right," Jackson said, taking the empty glass from her.

"We should open another bottle." Felicity stood. "There's got to be another one around here somewhere."

"Wait," Jackson said, getting to his feet. He was pleasantly buzzed, but certainly not to the point of slurring his words. "I'm thinking some decaf coffee or hot cocoa might be nice."

"But we don't have any Irish cream," Felicity whined as she walked into the kitchen, barely managing to avoid running into the doorframe.

Jackson chuckled softly as he followed her. "Maybe that's not a bad thing."

"Oh, *come on, Jackson.* Are you really saying you don't want to share another bottle of wine?"

"I'm just trying to save you from a hangover tomorrow," he said cheerfully. "Coffee or cocoa?"

Felicity sighed. "I suppose you're right." She flopped down at the table. "Coffee then. To go with the carrot cake in the fridge."

"Carrot cake. Is that what's in that box?" he asked as he prepared the coffee maker.

"Yeah." She propped her head up with one hand. "I stock the fridge with one for all my guests. It's the one thing that I do really well."

"Not the only thing," Jackson said with a wink.

Felicity's cheeks turned pink. "Are you flirting with me, Jackson Bell?"

"I thought that was obvious." After plating the carrot cake, he served them both and then took a seat next to her. He watched as she dug into the cake, closing her eyes and letting out a small moan. It was too much. He had to look away for fear he'd haul her off to the bedroom.

"Why are you the perfect man?" she asked, sounding frustrated.

"Perfect? I think you might be overstating things."

"No, I'm not," she said. "You're gorgeous. Thoughtful. Sensitive. A helluva good cook. And you're fun. I honestly don't know why some woman hasn't snatched you up yet."

"I've been wondering the same thing," he said as he held her gaze.

"Stop it. I'm never getting married."

"So you've said." He took a bite of the carrot cake and had to admit that it was delicious. "But no one ever said anything about marriage."

Felicity let out a scoff. "You did, too!"

"When?" He frowned at her.

"At Marissa and Danny's wedding. You pointed to your ring finger and told me that I'm next. Don't think I forgot about that."

"You thought I meant you were marrying me?" he asked with both eyebrows raised. "Presumptuous, don't you think?" Never mind the fact that she was the only person he'd met that he could see himself marrying. Still, that taunt had just been a joke.

"Are you saying you don't want to marry me?" she asked, looking annoyed.

"Are you proposing to me?" he teased.

Felicity threw her hands up, exasperated. "You're messing with me."

"Yes, just like I was at the wedding. Lighten up, Felicity. We haven't even been on our first date yet. Unless this counts."

"This isn't a date... I think." She shook her head. "Just because we had dinner and wine and carrot cake, that doesn't mean it's a date."

"How about the fire in the fireplace and the part where we share a bed?" he asked, completely amused.

"Whoa, whoa, whoa! Who said anything about sharing a bed?" She couldn't keep the smile off her lips, giving away her faux outrage. "I figured you'd sleep on the couch."

He shrugged. "If that's what you really want."

Felicity pushed her blond hair out of her eyes, blinked at him, and then shook her head. "You know that's not what I want."

He just grinned.

"Don't look so pleased with yourself." She forked in another bite of carrot cake. "You've just caught me at a vulnerable moment. First that scam loan paperwork, then the storm, and now—"

"What scam loan paperwork?" he asked, unsure if he'd missed something she'd said.

"That guy who handed me that envelope earlier." She sat up and pulled her hair back. "There was some bogus loan paperwork supposedly from over fifty years ago, stating that the loan, plus an outrageous amount of interest, has to be paid by the end of the year or else the property will be seized. I can't believe people fall for that crap. Either way, I'm giving it to my lawyer tomorrow to see if he can trace whoever is trying to pull this scam."

"A loan from fifty years ago? That certainly sounds sketchy," he said with a nod. "It's unusual to get something like that delivered on paper. These days it's usually just some vague email that is clearly written with AI tools."

"Yeah. I auto delete all that stuff. I guess the scammers are trying a little harder these days. There was even a copy of the loan with my grandmother's forged signature."

Alarm bells went off in Jackson's head. He'd worked in the corporate world in finance before he'd quit in order to live a quieter life. But during that time, he'd seen a number of strange business deals that had gone sideways due to outstanding liens and old contracts. He supposed it was possible that she was right, and someone was trying to scam her, but he'd feel better once her lawyer confirmed it. "Don't wait on that, okay? There was a known scam of people placing liens on deeds a while back, so make sure your lawyer checks with the assessor's office, too."

"Sure," she said, waving her hand. "But that's for tomorrow. Right now, I want to go make snow angels." Felicity stood and started walking toward the back door.

"Wait," he said, catching her hand before she walked out in just her socks. "You're hardly dressed for the snowy weather." He waved at her robe and fuzzy socks.

She looked down at herself and laughed. "Oops. I forgot." Then she eyed the frosted window and said, "Let me get my shoes, and we can catch snowflakes on our tongues instead."

Jackson shook his head but couldn't help being completely amused. Tipsy Felicity had let all her guards down and had forgotten to be cynical about life. It was as if all the weight of her responsibilities had lifted, and this carefree version of her was ready to just enjoy the moment.

"Okay, let's go," she said.

He looked down at her feet, noting the wet tennis shoes from earlier, and laughed. If she was going out, he certainly was, too. Jackson stuffed his feet back into his boots and then followed her outside.

Felicity ran into the fresh snow, letting out a shriek. "Oh my gosh! It's so cold. Burrrr."

Jackson walked up behind her and wrapped his arms around her waist. "Better?"

She leaned against him and nodded. Then she looked up at the falling snow, letting the flakes land on her face before she opened her mouth and stuck her tongue out. After tasting one, she turned in his arms and said, "Lucy's right. They need sugar."

"What?" he asked, staring at her in confusion.

"You know, Lucy from *Peanuts*. She says December snowflakes are too early and need sugar. But I know how to fix that." Her gaze landed on his lips before she leaned in and pressed her mouth to his.

The kiss was soft, tentative at first, but then Felicity opened her mouth and her tongue darted out, tasting him. He tightened his hold on her and deepened the kiss, hungry for more of her. The one night they'd spent together hadn't been enough. He'd been dreaming of having her in his arms ever since.

"Mmmm," she murmured when she pulled away. "Yeah, that's better."

Before he could answer, she stepped out of his embrace and then held her arms out to the side before she let herself fall backward into the snow. She let out a tiny cry of surprise as she landed and laughed as she made sure the robe was still wrapped tightly around her. Then she flung her arms out again before she started moving them back and forth.

"You're crazy, you know that?" he asked.

"Get down here with me, Jackson," she demanded. "You're missing all the fun."

Who was he to deny her anything she wanted? He stood near her, opened his arms, and let himself fall.

"Yes!" Felicity cried.

He moved his arms and legs, making the snow angel, and when he was done, he looked over at Felicity. Her eyes were closed and there was a small smile on her lips. He knew then that deep down, this was a woman who loved the Christmas season. That love was just buried underneath all the emotional wounds of the past.

"This was fun, Felicity," he said, slipping his hand over hers.

She opened her eyes and looked at him, her expression soft. "It was. I used to love snowstorms. It's when everything stops and suddenly the only thing to do is to spend time together until it's over."

"It looks to me like you still love them," he said.

"Well, yes, I suppose I do." She sat up, her body shivering now.

"We'd better get you inside before frostbite sets in." He got to his feet and held out a hand to her. She grabbed it with both of hers and used it to haul herself up. She slipped a little, pitching forward and grabbing onto his chest to keep from falling again.

He quickly steadied her, and once again they found themselves molded together.

"I think we better go inside," she whispered. "This time, I

think I'll let you warm me up instead of the shower." She slipped from his grip and hurried back inside the house.

Jackson stood there for a moment, the snowflakes still swirling around him as he tried to steel himself. There wasn't anyone he wanted more than Felicity Hill. But she'd been drinking. And as much fun as it was to play in the snow with her while she was slightly intoxicated, the next time he found himself being intimate with her, they were both going to be completely sober.

He took a step toward the house and then suddenly stopped as a flash of light caught his attention in the trees behind the cabin. Taking a step toward the tree line, he peered into the darkness, looking for whoever might be there.

Another twinkle of light flashed from his right. He walked toward it, feeling as if he was magically drawn to something. It wasn't until he got to the tree line that he heard it. There was a faint tinkling of bells, followed by what sounded like someone humming the tune "Silent Night."

"Who's there?" he asked.

The humming and the bells stopped, and utter silence rang in his ears.

"Hello?" he tried again.

"Over here," the inviting voice called.

Jackson hesitated for just a moment before he took a step into the woods. Suddenly the snow vanished. There were twinkling lights secured to the trees, and the voice was singing again. He spun, looking for the cabin, but it wasn't there. All he saw was the warm forest clearing that was full of Christmas lights and a crackling fire in the middle.

Despite the change in scenery and seemingly being cut off from the cabin, Jackson didn't feel threatened. Quite the contrary. He somehow knew that he'd been invited into a special magical realm, a place that had always existed but remained hidden for years at a time.

"Do you have a message for me?" he asked in a normal voice.

A few feet in front of him, light shimmered from seemingly nowhere until the most ethereal Christmas fairy appeared in front of him. She had long silver hair, a poinsettia flower pinned behind her ear, and was wearing a green velvet dress that was cinched with a piece of garland. When she spoke, her voice was like a warm hug, rich and inviting. "Good evening, Jackson Bell."

"Good evening," he said, in awe of the familiar vision in front of him. He had the distinct impression that they'd met before, but he had zero memory of it. "I'm sorry. I don't know your name."

"How could you? I've never given it to you." Her eyes twinkled with kindness. "You can call me Grace."

"Okay, Grace." He swallowed, sure that this was a once in a lifetime event. "Can you tell me what you are? A fairy or…"

"Yes. A Christmas Grove woodland fairy. I, along with my family, protect this land," she said kindly. "And the people who love it as much as we do."

"Are you saying you protect Felicity?" he asked.

The beautiful woodland fairy just smiled at him and said, "She's going to need you this season."

"Felicity?" he asked, wanting to make sure he didn't misunderstand her vague message.

She nodded. "In order to be sure that this land remains safe, you're going to need to help her find her Christmas spirit."

"I think we had a decent start tonight," he said, wondering if he was hallucinating.

"You did. That's how we know you're the right one for this mission. Remember, Jackson Bell, you're the chosen one to help Felicity remember the magic of Christmas." Her smile faded, and worry seeped into her brilliant blue eyes. "Otherwise, us fairies will cease to exist and the orchards will slowly die out."

"That's... dramatic, don't you think?" he asked.

The fairy shook her head and then faded away, taking the cozy surroundings with her.

He blinked, and suddenly he was just in a thicket of snow-covered trees. "Grace?" he called out.

Silence.

He glanced around, squinting through the snowflakes.

There was nothing to be seen but trees and snow. Had he just hallucinated? He couldn't help but wonder. But he really didn't think so. The interaction had just seemed far too real.

And really, what was the harm in doing what he could to help Felicity find her Christmas spirit? It was a job he'd gladly do.

Determined to take the message to heart, he turned around, spotted the lights glowing from the cabin, and headed back.

Felicity was waiting for him at the door. "What took you so long? Were you building a snowman without me?"

He chuckled. "No, but we'll do that first thing in the morning."

"Deal." Felicity grabbed his hand, and instead of leading him to the living room and the fireplace, she led him to the bathroom where she'd already started the hot water in the shower. She moved to untie the robe, but Jackson quickly put his hands over hers, stopping her.

"I don't think we should do this tonight," he said, squeezing her hands gently.

"I don't see why not." There was a sly smile on her face as she placed her hands on his chest and ran them over his pecs. "We're two consenting adults who don't have anything else to fill our time."

There wasn't anything he wanted more than to take her to bed and explore every inch of her. But the last time they'd been together, she'd been clear about it just being a one-time thing. And since she was obviously more than a little tipsy, he just couldn't take that step. "We've both been drinking," he said gently. "I don't want you to regret anything in the morning."

"Oh, I'm not going to regret anything," she said, shaking her head. "Not when it comes to you."

"You have no idea how much I like hearing that," he said.

"But I still think we should table this tension between us for another night. Unfortunately."

She let out an audible sigh. "Fine. I always did think you were maybe too much of a gentleman," she teased. "But we'll see if you change your mind once we're both in that bed."

Jackson swallowed hard. "I should probably sleep on the couch."

Felicity stared at him for a moment, and then right when she opened her mouth to answer him, there was an audible *boom*, and the lights went out. "Uh-oh. Power's out."

"Should we check the breakers?" he asked, though with the storm, he assumed it was a widespread outage.

"We can, but it's unlikely to change things," she said as she tapped the flashlight on her phone and then led him into the kitchen area before opening a door to a small laundry room. "The panel is on the left side."

Jackson took her phone, quickly checked the electrical panel, and then determined it wasn't a tripped breaker. "Looks like we're in the dark for the foreseeable future."

"You can forget that couch. The fireplace isn't going to keep the bedroom warm, and there are only a couple of extra blankets in the cabin," she said. "If we both want to keep warm, we're gonna need our shared body heat."

There was no arguing with that, so he just nodded and followed her back into the cold bedroom. She disappeared into the bathroom where the shower was still running.

Jackson found a couple of candles and lit them before stripping out of his wet clothes and hanging them in the closet, hoping they'd dry by morning. Then he wrapped himself in the second terrycloth robe and waited for her to finish in the bathroom.

When she finally came out, her long blond hair was tied up into a messy bun and her skin was rosy from the warm water. "Bathroom is all yours."

He hesitated, too taken in by her beauty to move.

Felicity chuckled softly. "If you keep looking at me like that, I think that gentlemanly resolve is going to fly right out the window."

She wasn't wrong. He nodded and disappeared into the bathroom. Ten minutes later, he reemerged, showered and teeth cleaned with the complimentary toothbrush that had been provided.

Felicity was curled up in the bed, the covers pulled up to her chin. He slipped in behind her, wrapping his arm around her completely naked body while he was in his boxer briefs.

"Sorry," she said softly. "I didn't have any pajamas."

"It's okay," he said hoarsely, desire intoxicating him. A full body shiver overtook him, and she snuggled her backside against him, probably assuming he was cold.

He carefully placed his hand on her bare stomach, closed his eyes, and prayed he'd make it through the night without mauling her.

CHAPTER 5

$\mathcal{F}$elicity woke with a slight pounding in her head. She let out a groan as she tried to roll over and collided with another body in her bed. Her eyes flew open, and she blinked hard at the unfamiliar surroundings.

"Good morning," the masculine voice said softly. "Did you sleep okay?"

She turned and spotted a very sexy sleepy-eyed Jackson Bell lying next to her. She blinked again as the memories of the night before started to flood back in. She grimaced. "Did I really run out into the snow in a robe to make snow angels?"

"You did." His eyes twinkled with amusement. "But you had fun."

"This headache says I had too much fun." She tossed the covers aside, gritted her teeth against the unbearable chill in the room, and quickly wrapped herself in the robe. After stuffing her feet into a pair of slippers, she hurried into the bathroom and shut the door, leaving her in the dark. She tried the light switch, only to realize the power was still out, and then raised the shade on the window, letting the morning light shine in.

Standing at the sink, she hung her head, trying to swallow the embarrassment she felt because of the way she'd acted the night before. She could still feel his hands clutching hers as he rejected her advances, and she felt both humiliated and grateful for his chivalry.

Exactly how much wine did she drink the night before? Not enough to be nauseated, but enough to invite the irritating headache and to make a fool of herself. She rummaged around in the cabinet and was grateful she had the foresight to keep the first aid kit stocked. After downing a couple of pain relievers, she washed her face, brushed her teeth, and then tried to tame her out-of-control hair.

Feeling a little better already, she steeled herself and walked back into the bedroom.

The bed was empty and the bedroom door was open. The air smelled of wood smoke, and she could hear the faint crackle of a fire in the fireplace.

She poked her head out of the bedroom and caught the scent of coffee coming from the kitchen. "Jackson Bell," she called out. "I do not deserve a friend like you. First a fire and now coffee?"

"Yes you do," he said as she walked into the kitchen. "It's what any sane person would do on a chilly morning." Jackson handed her a fresh mug of coffee. "I'm just thankful you have a gas stove and a French press, otherwise, we'd be up a creek without our caffeine."

Felicity held her mug up in a toast. "Grandma Kitty always said to be prepared for anything. I took that advice to heart."

"Thanks, Grandma Kitty."

They clinked mugs, and Felicity was pleased she'd managed to make Jackson smile. She still felt like a fool about the way she'd behaved the night before, but she was grateful he'd been a voice of reason when her inhibitions had left the building.

"Looks like the storm has passed. Does the farm have a snowplow attachment?" Jackson asked over his mug of coffee.

"Yes. It's in the shed next to the store," she said. "But Marilyn has the truck we use."

"I have a truck. Once we finish breakfast, we'll get it attached and I'll do my best to clear the snow from your road. And I'll see if there's a way to clear that tree. Do you have a chainsaw?"

"Of course. But you don't need to do any of that," she said, shaking her head. "It's my orchard. When the road is clear and Marilyn gets here, we'll take care of it."

He put his coffee mug down and crossed his arms over his chest as he leaned against the counter. "Is it always this hard for you to accept help?"

"No," she said automatically, but she knew that was a lie. She'd always been reluctant to lean on anyone, though it was hard to admit it. Life was just easier that way.

"So it's just me you don't want helping you then," he said, looking both hurt and annoyed.

"That's not—" She let out a groan. "It's not you. I don't like owing people anything or depending on other people. It never ends well for me."

"Trust issues then," he said, and before she could answer he added, "I'm going to plow the road unless you forbid me from using your equipment, and you're not going to owe me anything. Consider it my way of making sure I can get out of here so I can get to work tonight."

Why did this man always cut right through her crap? It was disconcerting. But he was right. They were both stuck at the orchard unless they cleared her private road. No one else was going to do it. "Okay, that's fair. But at least let me buy you dinner sometime for helping out."

"I'd tell you that's not necessary, but I'm not turning down an offer like that. It's a date." He winked and then turned to the stove where he'd already set out a pan and lit the burner beneath it. He glanced over his shoulder. "Fried egg sandwiches for breakfast?"

"Sounds good." She opened the fridge, grateful that the contents were still cold, and pulled out the eggs for him. "But it's not a date. It's a thank you."

"Whatever you want to call it," he said with an unconcerned shrug.

Felicity wanted to argue, but it was clear that whatever she said, he was still going to think of it as a date. Instead, she decided to drop it, hoping that once he realized she wasn't the dating type that he'd finally take the hint.

After breakfast, they bundled up and went out to Jackson's truck. Luckily the four-wheel drive was enough to get them back over to the store where they mounted the snowplow attachment.

"I can do this if you need to get the store ready to open," he said.

"You're not going to remove that fallen tree by yourself," she shot back. "I'm going with you. If you'll grab the chainsaw and gloves from the shed, I'll go inside and make sure the backup generator is running so the food in the freezers doesn't spoil." While the cabin didn't have a generator, the store did. They had months' worth of frozen apples and pies to keep them going after the holiday season. If those spoiled, she'd be in a world of hurt.

"On it," he said.

They parted ways. Felicity checked the store and was pleased to see that the generator had come on exactly as it should. Once she was satisfied the store was in good shape, she returned to the truck to find Jackson loading the back with the chainsaw, a handsaw, a shovel, protective gear, and her rawhide gloves.

"Ready?" he asked.

"As ready as I'm gonna be," she said and climbed into the passenger seat.

He joined her and then put the truck in gear. After running the plow up and down the long driveway a few times, Jackson turned onto the county road and plowed the snow until he reached the bridge.

Felicity grimaced when she saw the tree still blocking the entrance. "That's gonna take a while."

"Have you used a chainsaw before?" he asked her.

"Of course I have," she said, almost insulted. "The one in the back of your truck is mine, isn't it?"

He held his hands up in surrender. "I wasn't sure if you had a groundskeeper who did that work for you. I was going to suggest that you make the cuts and I'll move the logs to the side of the road. Or we can haul it back to your cabin for firewood."

She eyed the tree. It was a fairly large size, but not impossible. If a redwood tree had fallen, that would be another story. This one appeared to be some sort of oak tree, which meant it would be heavy to lift. "Yeah, okay."

Together they decided where it was best to cut the tree. And then after Felicity put on her eye protection and gloves, she fired up the chainsaw and got to work. The vibration made her arms shake, but she'd done enough trimming in the orchard over the years that she was able to make the cuts without incident. Sweat had broken out on her forehead, and the ache in her forearms was more than she'd bargained for. Once she killed the engine on the saw, she forced herself to take it back to the truck and place it in the bed. Then she let out a moan as she shook out her arms, wondering if she'd even be able to lift them later.

"Are you all right?" Jackson asked her as he bent at the knees and lifted one of the logs.

"I'll be fine," she said, unwilling to voice just how much her arms ached.

He nodded and went back to moving the pieces of the tree. When he was finally finished, he was winded and sat right down in the snow, rolling his shoulders to work the kinks out.

"I don't think either of us is in good enough shape for hard labor," Felicity said.

"Speak for yourself," Jackson said, feigning offense. "I'm ready to go mountain climbing."

"Yeah, your beet-red face says otherwise," Felicity said with a laugh.

He chuckled. "I admit to nothing."

Felicity looked around at the road and smiled. "Once we plow the road to the highway, we'll be good to go."

"You're right." He held a hand out to her. "Help me up and we'll get on that."

She braced herself so that she wouldn't slip on the wet snow and helped him to his feet. Together, they walked back to the truck to finish the job. Luckily, when they got to the highway, the plows had already gone through.

When they got back to Apples and Spice and Everything Nice, Felicity was pleased to see that the power had already come back on. It looked like everyone was going to be able to get on with their day.

After they put the tools away in the shed, Felicity turned to Jackson to thank him one more time, but when she found him crouching in the snow, she asked, "What are you doing now?"

"Making good on that snowman idea we had last night." He grinned up at her. "Are you helping or watching?"

"I don't—"

"Oh no, you're not backing out now," he said. "I'm not leaving until this thing is done. A promise is a promise."

She didn't remember him promising anything, but she could tell by the determination in his face that she wasn't going to win this one. "Fine. I'll go rummage up some adornments for its face. I'll be right back."

"Take your time. I'll just be here working on the body," he said with a cheerful wave.

Shaking her head at his relentless energy, Felicity went inside the shop and into her office to look through a box of holiday decorations. They used to do a snowman building contest back when she was younger. She knew there were some things lying around that would spruce up Jackson's creation.

As she was digging around in the box, the phone buzzed. When she saw Marilyn's name flash on the screen, she answered. "You must have made it through the storm all right."

"I did, but what about you? Did you make it home?" her friend asked.

"Nope. A tree went down, blocking the bridge. I stayed in the cabin." She didn't mention the part about Jackson being with her. It wasn't that she didn't trust Marilyn, she just didn't want to have to explain herself. "Our guests got stuck and couldn't get up the mountain, and since I'd stocked the fridge for them, I had enough for dinner and breakfast. The power went out, but it's already back on."

"That was lucky," she said. "I was going to get on the road, but if there's a tree down—"

"It's already cleared," Felicity said.

"Seriously? The road crews must really be on their game," she said, sounding astonished. "They're never that fast."

She was right. They weren't. And if she told her that she had taken care of it, she'd have to tell her about Jackson, so Felicity just agreed with her and said, "There's no hurry to come in anyway. No one is out yet. I'm just gonna do some paperwork and clean up around here before I head home for a change of clothes."

"Okay, I'll grab donuts on my way and some deli sandwiches for lunch since it's Friday," Marilyn said. "That's mainly why I called. To let you know what I chose for lunch. Do you want your regular?"

"Definitely. Roast beef with swiss and a side of country potato salad." Felicity's mouth watered at just the thought of her favorite sandwich. After doing manual labor all morning, her breakfast was long gone.

"Perfect. I'll see you later."

After Felicity hit End on her phone, she spotted the manila envelope on her desk and groaned. She didn't want to deal with the bogus scam but knew it was better to tackle it head on. She scrolled through her phone contacts until she found the lawyer her grandmother had always used and then tapped the button to connect.

The call went straight to voice mail.

If Felicity had to guess, he probably wasn't in his office yet after the storm. She ended the call and fired up her computer instead. After sending him an email with scans of the paperwork, she went back to the Christmas decoration box.

Finally, she found the canvas bag she was looking for in the very bottom. Without even inspecting the contents, she swung it over her shoulder and went back outside to help Jackson with the snowman.

To her surprise, he was already working on the second ball for his body. "You're fast."

He grinned up at her. "I spent a lot of time in the snow as a kid."

"That seems obvious." She put the canvas bag down and got to work on making the snowman's head. After a while, she stared at the lumpy head and said, "Listen, Frank, you behave, or all the customers are gonna think you have brain damage."

Jackson chuckled. "Frank?"

"Frosty's second cousin who prefers football over ice skating," she said. "See this lump? He got it after he was tackled one too many times." She grinned at him.

Jackson grinned back at her. "Careful. One might think you're actually enjoying yourself."

"Never." She winked at him.

He looked far too pleased with himself, so she went back to work on shaping Frank's head.

A few minutes later, Jackson said, "I think we're ready for lump-head Frank now."

Felicity eyed his snowman and was super impressed

with how symmetrical he'd managed to get the two balls of snow that made up the body. She looked at Frank. He still had a lump, but if she put that side down where his head connected to the body, nobody but she and Jackson would know. "Okay, let's do it."

With Jackson's help, they positioned the head and then stood back admiring their handiwork.

"Not bad, if I do say so myself," Jackson said.

"It's perfect," she agreed. "Or it will be once he gets his eyes and scarf." Felicity retrieved the canvas bag, pulled out the scarf, and then fished around for the buttons she knew had to be there. Her hand wrapped around something round and smooth. "Ah-ha! There's one. I knew—"

She stared down at the golden apple pin in her hand, remembering the day her grandmother had added it as a nose for her snowman when no one could find a carrot. Instead of being the gut-punch she was expecting, all she felt was joy at the memory.

"What is it?' Jackson asked gently, obviously knowing she'd found something significant.

"It's Frank's nose," she said, holding it up. "Instead of a button nose, it's an apple nose."

Jackson smiled at her. "Seems perfect."

"It is." Felicity dug around, found the buttons, and then attached them both for eyes before positioning the apple nose. Jackson wrapped the scarf around his neck, and when they were done, they stood back, admiring their creation. Felicity pursed her lips. "He needs a mouth."

"Do you have Red Vines in the store?" he asked.

"Yes! Oh my gosh. That's perfect." She ran inside, found the candy, and was out in a flash. When she got there, she found that Jackson had fished a knitted cap out of his truck and had attached it to Frank's head. "Nice touch," she said as she added the Red Vine for the mouth.

"Perfect," Jackson said, stepping back to admire their creation. "And no lumpy head in sight. No one but us has to know he has brain damage."

Felicity cackled. "I won't tell a soul."

"Me neither." He walked over to her, brushed his lips over her cheek, and said, "I'll call you about that date."

Felicity watched as Jackson climbed into his truck. She felt a tiny pang of regret, not wanting him to leave just yet. She hated to admit it, even to herself, but she'd had a good time last night and this morning. Why was it she wouldn't date him again?

Oh, right. He was a commitment guy.

She wasn't.

Sighing, Felicity grabbed the canvas bag and headed back into the store. Her temporary winter break was over. It was time to work.

CHAPTER 6

"How ow was your evening?" Marissa called out as Jackson walked into Sleighed that afternoon.

"Good," he said. "You?"

"That's all I get? Good?" Marissa asked as she hurried over to him, giving him a knowing look. "You spent all night with Felicity, In a snowstorm, and all you've got is 'good.' You have to give me more than that."

He shook his head at his boss, who also happened to be one of Felicity's best friends. "What kind of gentleman would I be if I said more?"

The fiery redhead let out a small gasp as she bounced on the balls of her feet. "Are you saying you don't kiss and tell?"

"I didn't say anything about kissing," he said.

"Ugh! You're the worst. You're not giving me anything at all." She threw her hands up in exasperation. "Everyone knows you two are meant for each other. Just put me out of my misery already. Did you get together or not?"

"We did not get together," he said, slightly frustrated that he couldn't give her a different answer.

"Oh. Well, that's disappointing," she said as she leaned against the bar. "I was hoping that she'd finally let her guard down."

She had, but Jackson wasn't going to give Marissa those details. If Felicity wanted her to know, she could tell her later. "I'm going to get to work."

"Yeah, okay. But I still want all the details later," she called as he slipped into the kitchen.

"Never gonna happen!" he called back.

Marissa let out a fake cry of frustration and then cackled.

Jackson shook his head and got busy prepping for dinner.

By the time nine o'clock rolled around, Jackson's back was aching and he was starving. It had been fairly busy. Apparently being snowed in for one night in Christmas Grove had been too much for the locals. They'd all come out to blow off some steam while they indulged in wings and gourmet burgers. After fixing both him and Marissa plates of food, he shut down the kitchen and then walked out into the bar.

"Guacamole burger or black and blue burger?" Jackson asked her, holding both plates.

"Black and blue," she said, taking the blue cheese burger from him. "I've been craving this all week."

"I know," he said as he winked and then took a seat at the bar next to Danny, her husband. There was already a glass of his favorite beer waiting for him.

"She's been talking about that burger for over a week," Danny said. "Ever since the last time you offered them but then sold out and she didn't get one."

"Yeah, she mentioned that once or twice," Jackson said with a chuckle. It had been more like every day for a week, but who was counting.

Marissa took a huge bite of her burger, closed her eyes, and moaned her satisfaction. Once she swallowed, she gave Jackson two thumbs-up and then put the plate under the counter as she went to serve drinks to more of her patrons.

Jackson had just taken a bite of his burger when Danny said, "I heard you spent the night with Felicity."

He sucked in a breath, got a piece of burger caught in this throat, and then started choking.

"Oh, dammit! Sorry." Danny started pounding on his back.

Jackson's eyes started to water, and just when he was certain he was going to die by burger, Danny wrapped his arms around him from behind and did a poor version of the Heimlich maneuver. The chunk of burger flew across the bar, and Jackson sucked in a breath of air. "Thank you," he wheezed.

"Marissa never would have forgiven me if I just sat here and watched her favorite chef choke to death." The words were teasing, but Danny's expression was full of concern. "Are you okay?"

"Yeah. Fine now." He picked up the beer and took a few gulps, grateful for the cold beverage.

"Remind me to never ask about Felicity when you're eating," Danny said.

"It's fine. I just sucked in too much air while I was chewing." He drank some more of his beer and then said, "Felicity and I were snowed in at her cabin last night. Nothing happened, so there's nothing to report, though I did help her plow her road this morning and remove a tree that was blocking the bridge."

Danny studied him for a moment and then nodded. "That sounds about right."

"What's that mean?" Jackson asked with a laugh.

"Just that you care about her and that scares her."

Jackson knew he was right, but chose to remain silent. He picked up his burger and took another bite. This time he managed to get it down without incident. When he was done with his dinner, he turned to Danny. "How's the pottery business?"

"Great. Busy for the Christmas season," his friend said. "After the New Year, Marissa and I are going to take a little getaway for our honeymoon."

They'd gotten remarried a few weeks ago at their new farmhouse after reconnecting during the previous Christmas season. But neither had wanted to take time off to travel after the ceremony since the holidays were when they were both busiest.

"Marissa wants somewhere warm with a swim up bar." He chuckled. "Gotta say I'm looking forward to whatever bikini she plans to wear. I love snow and Christmas, but I won't say no to a little bit of sunbathing in January."

"It does sound good," Jackson agreed, though he'd personally rather spend time on a ski slope than in a pool. Maybe he'd change his mind if Felicity wanted to vacation with him in the tropics.

The bells over the door chimed, and in walked none other than Felicity herself. She yanked off a knitted cap and stalked over to the bar. As she took a seat right in front of Marissa, she said, "You are not going to believe the day I had."

"Uh-oh. That doesn't sound good. Did the Christmas lights go out again?" Marissa asked.

"Oh," Felicity huffed out. "If only."

Marissa nodded at the taps. "Want one?"

"Yes. And keep them coming." She pulled off her gloves and made a pile of her outerwear on the stool next to her. "You are never going to believe this."

Jackson couldn't help but lean in to listen. He hated that her day had gone downhill after he'd left that morning. The time they'd spent together had felt nothing short of magical to him and had sustained him for the rest of the day. That clearly hadn't been the case for her.

"Okay, don't keep me in suspense," Marissa said. "Who do we need to hex?"

"Some old bastard who's trying to steal the orchard." Felicity scowled. "Yesterday afternoon I was served with some paperwork."

"Served? Like a lawsuit?" Marissa asked as she placed a Christmas Ale in front of her friend.

"Foreclosure paperwork." She picked up the beer and took a long swig. "There's been a lien placed on the orchard, and if I don't pay the loan plus interest, they're going to foreclose in the new year."

"What loan?" Marissa asked.

"You mean that wasn't a scam?" Jackson asked.

Felicity turned to him. All of her anger seemed to vanish, and her eyes turned haunted as she said, "My lawyer says it's legit. He says the lien was placed on the deed the week after that paperwork was signed... Decades ago."

Jackson wanted to pull her into his arms, comfort her, but when anger came flooding back into her expression as she straightened her shoulders, he knew that was the last thing she needed.

"What are you going to do?" Marissa asked. "Is there any way to come up with the money to pay off the loan?"

"The loan? Yes. The interest? No. I just don't understand it. My grandmother would have never left an outstanding debt like that," Felicity said, shaking her head with frustration. "She was so proud that she owned that land. The way she talked about it being her legacy for the Hill family, I just don't understand how there could be an outstanding loan. It makes no sense. Marilyn said she didn't know anything about it either."

"What can we do, honey?" Marissa asked, her tone full of compassion.

"Nothing. I don't know." She let out a sigh. "The lawyer is trying to track down the person who holds the lien. Maybe we can get answers then." Felicity tightened her grip on her beer and then downed the rest of it. "Okay. Enough of that. There's nothing I can do tonight, so who's drinking with me?"

"I am," Jackson said and moved to sit next to her.

She gave him a dazzling smile. "How did I know I could count on you?"

The memory of the woodland fairy he'd met on her property flashed in his mind. What was it she'd said? *In order to be sure that this land remains safe, you're going to need to help her find her Christmas spirit.* He wasn't sure that drinking her worries away was the best way to start that mission, but it was what he had to work with.

"Here you go," Marissa said with a soft chuckle as she placed two new beers in front of them. "What about you, Danny? Are you going to join them?"

Her husband shook his head. "Not tonight. I have a pottery class to teach tomorrow at the gallery."

"Way to be the adult in the room," Felicity said to him with a teasing tone. "I hope Marilyn can take care of the store by herself tomorrow. 'Cause I plan to be sleeping off a hangover." She lifted her glass and held it up for Jackson. "To blowing off steam."

He repeated her toast, clinked his glass to hers, and then took a sip.

She did the same and then looked at Jackson. "I assume since you're out here drinking that the kitchen is closed?"

"It is," he said. "But I can grab you a sandwich and some potato salad if you want."

"You, Jackson Bell, are once again my hero. If you feed me, I'm going to be your devoted servant forever."

"Servant isn't exactly the role I was hoping for," he said. "But if you'll indulge me, I'd love to get you on one of those horseless carriage rides."

"The one that takes everyone around to see the magical Christmas decorations?" she scoffed, looking slightly horrified.

"That's the one. How about a deal? I'll make you dinner and be your drinking buddy if you promise to let me take you around town in a carriage." He raised an eyebrow in challenge. "What do you say? Are you game?"

She looked around at the sparsely populated bar and said, "Looks like my options are limited, so I'm all yours."

If only, he thought ruefully. He raised his beer again. "Okay. Let the drinking commence."

Felicity grinned at him. "Now we're talking."

CHAPTER 7

*F*elicity hadn't had nearly enough beer for this. The last time she'd been cozied up in one of the horseless carriages that roamed Christmas Grove, she'd been a teenager. Handsy Harrison had been her date, and after the first sloppy kiss that was more saliva than tongue, she spent the rest of the night fending him off.

The memory was so vile that she found herself scowling as Jackson placed the thick blanket over their legs.

"What's wrong?" he asked as he pulled the blanket back. "Too warm?"

"Oh no." She reached for the blanket as the chill in the air set into her bones. "The blanket is perfect. I was just remembering a particularly unpleasant evening in one of these rolling cheeseball contraptions when I was in high school."

"Cheeseball contraption?" he asked with a chuckle and small shake of his head. "What's next? Is the tree-lighting ceremony at the square each year trite? Do you throw tomatoes at the screen if a Hallmark movie comes on? Do you leave coal for Santa?"

Felicity cackled. He seemed so earnest, but she knew he was just needling her. "No. Maybe. And no. I'm all for people enjoying the season any way they like. Even if it's riding around in one of these and marveling at the decorations. Maybe I'm the problem."

"I wouldn't say you're a problem. People like what they like," he said, resting his arm on the seat behind her as the carriage lurched forward. "But even if this is cheesy, there's nothing wrong with cheese."

"You know what, Jackson Bell?" she said, eyeing him with appreciation. "You're right about that. I love a good gouda. Now, show me some gourmet decorations."

He leaned forward and spoke as if talking to an invisible horse. "Show us the most interesting and unusual magical decorations that Christmas Grove has to offer."

"Uh-oh. Seems like we're in for some serious shenanigans," Felicity said, wondering exactly how long she'd be trapped in the carriage. Though, she did have to admit that sitting under a blanket with Jackson was hardly a hardship. She leaned into him, pressing her head to his shoulder, and was pleased when his arm tightened around her. After the day she'd had, she reveled in the warmth and safety of his embrace.

Felicity knew that snuggling with a man who made her feel safe certainly wasn't going to fix any of her problems, but Jackson had a way of making her feel comforted, and that was really what she needed at the moment. Otherwise, she was going to spend the rest of the night worrying about what was going to happen to her orchard.

"I'm not sure if magical snow is unusual, but that sure is pretty," Jackson said.

Felicity jerked her head up and turned to see what he was looking at. The carriage had stopped in front of a horse property that had a gentle, rolling landscape. At the end of a treelined drive sat a large white house that was lit up with what seemed to be twinkle lights, but when they blinked off, the lights all shot off the house and lined up in formation just before they darted into the shape of a Christmas tree.

"Are they fireflies?" Jackson asked. "Seems too cold for them though."

"They are snow fairies," Felicity said, her voice hushed with awe. "I've only seen them once before."

Jackson turned his attention to her. "I've never heard of snow fairies."

"They don't perform for just anyone. They must have a connection to someone who lives at that house." The fairies dispersed, and when they came back together, they formed a star. "Aren't they beautiful?"

"Extremely," he agreed. "When and where did you see them before?"

"With my grandmother," she said, pressing her hand to her heart. "One year when my mom went away for a weekend with her boyfriend when I was just sixteen, the snow fairies made an appearance at the orchard. It was mid-December, and they formed all kinds of holiday images, but at the end, they formed an apple. I'll never forget it."

"Like they are now?" Jackson asked softly.

Felicity's eyes widened and then filled with tears as the snow fairies held an apple formation. And when they started to hum Silent Night, a single tear rolled down her cheek. She was so moved that she felt like her heart was going to burst. "Thank you," she whispered to the fairies. "You have no idea what you've given me."

The humming faded and then suddenly the fairies disappeared. Snow began to drift down over the gorgeous property, turning it into something out of a Christmas card. Felicity clutched at Jackson's hand, full of love and warm memories. She looked up at him. "How did you make this happen?"

"I didn't," he said, running his hand down her arm. "I had no idea that snow fairies even exist. All I did was ask that this carriage ride be something special. I guess this means mission accomplished."

Felicity let out a bark of delighted laughter, almost unable to believe she was actually having a good time. It had been years since she'd enjoyed anything to do with Christmas. Not because she didn't want to, but because it had hurt too much. Now, somehow, the sweet man beside her had just found a way to give her back something that she'd lost when her grandmother passed. That joy when the magic of Christmas touched her. He could never understand what that meant to her. She smiled up at him.

"This was just our first stop. I can hardly wait to see what else is in store for us."

"You and me both," Jackson said as he stared at the snow-blanketed house, awe in his handsome features.

As gorgeous as the farm was, Felicity found herself studying Jackson's face. There was a sense of wonder about him that she couldn't deny was infectious. Everything about him was at ease, but he also seemed to still have that childlike joy bubbling beneath the surface. It was charming, as well as a little disarming, to realize that the joy was part of why she was so drawn to him.

He tore his eyes away from the farm and then met hers. Electricity sparked between them, and Felicity sucked in a tiny breath as a shiver sparked over her skin. Jackson took it as the invitation it was and bent to kiss her. His lips were warm and demanding as his arms tightened around her. She reached up, sliding her fingers through his thick dark hair as she leaned into him, getting lost in the kiss.

Jackson caressed her cheek as he pulled back and said, "If we don't stop, we're going to be giving the snow fairies quite the show."

Felicity chuckled softly. "We wouldn't want to scandalize them."

"I'm more worried about frostbite if we start ripping each other's clothes off."

"I'm not." She winked at him, knowing that if he got her clothes off, she'd be burning up from the inside out. But she was still a respected member of Christmas Grove. She figured she'd like to keep it that way.

"You're trouble," he said and then asked the carriage to carry on.

The carriage moved effortlessly down one of the country roads until it suddenly stopped by a large frozen pond. There weren't any houses nearby, and the moon was shining down on the icy surface.

"What are we supposed to be looking at?" Felicity asked.

"I'm not—oh." Jackson pointed to the other side of the pond. "Look."

Out of the shadows, suddenly a dozen snowmen appeared and stepped out onto the ice in ice skates. They lined up, skating around, and then suddenly broke out in what could only be described as a flash mob. "All I Want for Christmas is You" started to play out of nowhere, and the snowmen started spinning and jumping while one did fancy footwork as if he were a professional ice dancer. Snowmen were everywhere, delighting Felicity.

She couldn't help it. She started to dance in her seat as she sang along with the song that usually grated on her nerves due to how much it was overplayed in every establishment in Christmas Grove. But the dancing was so good, she just couldn't be anything but joyful.

"Wow," Jackson said after one of them did a back flip that turned into a spin that was so fast the snowman became just a white blur in the middle of the pond.

The rest of the snowmen danced around, tipping their hats and skating as gracefully as Olympic ice skaters. Suddenly the snowmen and the music stopped. One by one the snowmen left the pond, leaving only the one right in the middle, who was still frozen in his post-spin pose.

The moon seemed to shine brighter, and suddenly the polished snowman morphed into something more rustic. A snowman that looked all too familiar. One that had been built in front of her store that morning.

The snowman moved its stick arm to its face, touched its glass apple nose, and then pointed at Felicity and Jackson before turning and skating off the pond.

"Are you sure you didn't plan this?" Felicity asked Jackson with suspicion.

"Scout's honor," he said, holding up three fingers. "I figured you'd stop by while I was still working in the kitchen. You usually don't come in so late."

Most days she popped in to say hi to Marissa, but even she had to admit that she didn't stay for a beer that often. She usually had a diet soda while she caught up with her friend, and then she headed home to have dinner with her roommate, Clara. "Okay, but you still could have planned this."

"While I'd love to take credit for this, I can't," he said. "We'll just have to chalk it up to some Christmas Grove holiday magic."

"Okay. If you say so," Felicity said, even though she still wasn't one hundred percent sure he hadn't had anything to do with all the specific details. But then, he hadn't even known that snow fairies existed, had he? She supposed he could have been acting, but she really didn't think so.

The carriage rolled on, taking them to the town square

where all the twinkle lights just happened to be in the shape and color of golden apples. The scent of warm apple pie filled the air, and as they passed the large Christmas tree in the center of the square, paper cups appeared out of thin air, hovering right in front of both of them. There were two peppermint sticks poking out of the whipped cream that covered the top of her cup. Jackson's only had one.

The image of her grandmother adding a second stick to her peppermint hot chocolate flashed in her mind, and just like that, she knew without a doubt that Jackson hadn't planned this evening.

Her grandmother had.

She didn't know how or why. But she did know that somehow her sweet grandmother had found a way to contact her from the other side to let her know that she was still with her. That whatever happened with the orchard, she was still there watching over Felicity.

"Jackson?" she asked, meeting his gaze.

"Yes?"

"You used to work in the business world, right? Something to do with real estate?" Her heart was pounding as she opened herself up to the man beside her. It had been forever since she'd really started to trust someone new, but it seemed that her grandmother had used Jackson to reach her, and that was good enough for Felicity.

"Not exactly real estate, though that was involved," he said. "I was a VP for Snow Valley Sports. I did a lot of work on new store openings and mergers when the company took over smaller sports stores that were struggling. Once deals were reached, I dealt with the details of making sure everything went smoothly without any legal issues popping up later."

"That's what I thought," she said with a nod. "So tracking down the person who holds the lien on the orchard shouldn't be too hard for you, right?"

He shrugged one shoulder. "It really depends on what's on the filed paperwork, but it shouldn't be too hard. Unless it's registered to shell company after shell company, designed to protect the identity of an individual, the name can always be found, but it sometimes takes time."

"Time I don't have," she said. "But you'll try anyway?"

"Of course. But what about your lawyer?" Jackson asked. "Doesn't he have people on staff who can do that?"

"Staff?" Felicity let out a humorless laugh. "Charlie has an assistant who answers his phone and files his paperwork. But she's even older than him, and he's nearing seventy. While they are adept at knowing what to file to keep my business legal and up to date, they aren't exactly investigators. He told me he checked with the county today, and the paperwork lists an LLC that's based in Delaware, so there's no way to find out who owns it. At least not quickly."

"I can definitely help you with that," he said. "All you need to do is get me a copy of the lien as well as the foreclosure notice, and I'll get right on it," he said.

Relief flooded through her, and for the first time since her lawyer told her that the paperwork looked legit, she started to feel some hope. If she could just talk to whoever was behind the loan, she might have a chance to save her family land. "I think you're too good to be true, Jackson Bell. It seems that in the past thirty-six hours you've become a sort of knight-in-shining armor."

"This is just what friends do," he said, rolling his eyes playfully at her. "I'm happy to help."

She leaned into him again and said, "If I ever forget to tell you thank you, just know that I'm forever grateful."

He squeezed her hand and then told the carriage to carry on.

When the carriage stopped in front of her house nearly an hour later, Felicity spied her Jeep in the driveway. "How did that get there?"

"I had Danny and Marissa bring it back for you. I figured after all the drinking, neither of us should be driving," he said.

While she supposed that was true, neither of them had actually had that much beer, and it had been hours since their last drink. She wasn't in any way intoxicated. Well, not unless one counted the way she felt when she looked at Jackson. And for once, it had nothing to do with the way he looked, though that certainly didn't hurt. But no, this time it was because he'd brought her something she'd been missing in her life for years. A little bit of Christmas magic. It made her head spin a little.

She sat in the carriage looking at the small house that she shared with Clara. The lights were out except for the twinkling tree that was in the front window. The tree that Clara must have decorated the night before and put up by herself. There was also a pretty homemade wreath on the front door along with a red ribbon that had been strung to make it look like the door was a present itself.

"Looks like we're not the only ones who found a little Christmas cheer," Jackson said.

"Clara's been busy," she agreed. Then Felicity laughed. "I bet Clara's worried I'm going to be a Grinch. Like usual."

"And will you be?" he asked, eyeing her with curiosity.

"Not tonight. Tomorrow? No promises." She leaned in, gave him a slow gentle kiss on his lips, and then hopped out of the carriage. "Thank you for the wonderful evening, Jackson. I'll come by your place in the morning with that paperwork you asked for."

"I'm looking forward to it," he said.

Felicity watched as the carriage rolled down her street, presumably taking Jackson to his house. It wasn't until the carriage rounded the corner that she finally turned and walked into her own home, silently berating herself for not inviting him in.

Clara was already in bed, so she crept into the kitchen, smiled at the Christmas cookies her friend had made, and then grabbed a bottle of water before retreating to her bathroom, where she climbed into a hot bubble bath and smiled to herself as she closed her eyes and relaxed for what seemed like the first time in forever.

CHAPTER 8

*J*ackson sat in his sunroom with a cup of coffee, looking out at the mountain. It was the entire reason he'd purchased his home after moving to Christmas Grove. It was the only room on the third story of his modest two-bedroom cottage, and because of that, it had a 360-degree view. One direction was the mountain he loved so much. The other overlooked the river and the charming town itself.

Because of all his time spent skiing down mountains before he'd hurt his knee, the mountain was what made him feel most at home.

Or at least it had been until he'd met Felicity Hill.

Last night had been nothing short of miraculous. He hadn't really thought he'd get her into one of the magical carriages that took people around to see Christmas decorations. He'd considered it a win just to convince her to go with him. But the moment the snow fairies showed up, he knew there was magic involved. He imagined that the woodland fairies had sent them, but he really wasn't sure. All he knew was that he was happy he'd been there when Felicity needed him.

And today he was going to make good on his promise to help her track down whoever was behind the loan on her orchard. Maybe he could even help her make a deal that would clear the debt and make all the legal trouble go away. He just needed to find out what the people behind the lien really wanted and then find a way to make it happen.

He'd just gone downstairs to refill his coffee mug when his doorbell rang. He quickly glanced at the clock. It was seven-thirty. He hadn't imagined that Felicity would show up quite that early, but a smile broke out over his lips as he went to the door.

"Missed me, did you?" he asked as he swung the door open. But when he saw the person on his porch, his smile vanished and he frowned. "Eva? What are you doing here?"

"Jackson," Eva Bell *tsked*. "Is that any way to greet your mother?" She stepped closer as she opened her arms wide. "Give your old mom a hug."

On autopilot, Jackson did as he was told, giving her a quick, awkward hug. But then he stepped back again, putting some much-needed distance between them. He cleared his throat and tried again. "What are you doing in Christmas Grove?"

"Can't a mother just come see her son for Christmas without twenty questions?" She picked up the bag she'd set at her feet and then swept past him into his house. "I presume that the guest room is free?"

No! "Yes," he said reluctantly. While he didn't have a great relationship with his mother, it wasn't bad enough that he'd force her to get a room at the inn. And since Christmas Grove was a popular destination during the entire month of December, it was unlikely the inn had any rooms anyway. He shut the door and turned to her. "How long do you plan on staying?"

"Through Christmas of course. That's not a problem, is it?" She smiled sweetly at him. "I thought it would be fun to take that glass blowing class together. I never did get around to using that gift certificate you got me."

The one he'd purchased after she told him over and over again how much she'd always wanted to learn how to make pretty pumpkins and Christmas ornaments. But two days after he'd given it to her, she'd packed up and left with barely an explanation. She'd said something about running off to LA for an audition. One he assumed she hadn't gotten since she hadn't told him about it.

His mother was an actress who'd starred in a sitcom many years ago. Since then she'd had very minor roles in various shows and movies, but her stage name had faded from the spotlight so long ago that almost no one recognized her anymore. Last he'd heard, she'd been working as a stylist for a reality show. He thanks the gods every day that she hadn't managed to be cast on the show herself.

"The show is on hiatus, and I had some time, so I

thought, why not come to Christmas Grove?" she said with a cheerful smile. "Surprise!"

He tried to keep the scowl off his face as he looked at her overnight bag. "Is that all you brought?"

"Oh, no. My bags are in the rental car. Would you mind getting them for me while I freshen up?" She walked to the hallway and then stopped and looked back at him. "Which one is the guest room again?"

The desire to roll his eyes was strong. She had stayed there for just over a week when she'd visited last time. It wasn't as if his house was a giant mansion. There were two bedrooms. His was hard to miss considering it was the primary with an en suite bathroom on the second floor, while the guestroom was on the main level. "The one at the end of the hall. The bathroom is right next to it."

"That's right," she said with a nod. "I suppose you didn't get around to remodeling so that the bedroom and bathroom are connected, did you?"

"No, I did not," he said and then strode out the door to find her luggage.

"Jackson, your girlfriend is here," Eva called from the back door.

He looked up at his mother. She looked so foreign wearing one of his kitchen aprons over her silk blouse and designer jeans. There was a smudge of flour on her cheek, and if things were different between them, he'd have found her charming.

Instead, he was just annoyed that she was messing up his kitchen, pretending to recreate memories they definitely didn't have.

"Jackson?" she called again. "Did you hear me?"

He leaned the axe against the wood pile and called back. "Yes. I'll be there in a second." There hadn't actually been a need for him to split logs. He had enough to last him for at least a month, but the nervous energy that had settled in when his mother insisted on making Christmas cookies had sent him outdoors. He removed his work gloves, shoved his hair back, and went inside.

Felicity was standing just inside the kitchen door, her eyebrows raised as she glanced between him and Eva. "Jackson, you didn't tell me your mother was in town."

"She just got here this morning." He placed his hand on her elbow and gently guided her toward the stairs. "Let's go talk in my office."

"Jackson, aren't you going to introduce us?" Eva called out just as they got to the stairs.

He glanced at Felicity. "She didn't introduce herself when she let you in?"

"She did," Felicity said with a soft chuckle. "Although I told her my name, I didn't give her any more details. I think she's fishing to see if I might be a possible daughter-in-law candidate. I heard that girlfriend comment, which you didn't contradict by the way."

"I'll correct her later," Jackson said, hating the idea of

telling his mother anything about his private life. They didn't have that kind of relationship. They barely had any relationship at all.

He led her up to the sunroom on the third floor and closed the door behind them.

Felicity walked over to the windows that faced the mountain and let out a low whistle. "Great view."

"It's why I bought the place."

"No doubt." She walked to the other side and stared down at Christmas Grove. "It really does look like something out of a Norman Rockwell painting, doesn't it?"

Jackson chuckled softly. "I don't recall ever seeing any bars in those paintings."

"I'm sure there was a speakeasy hiding behind a toy store or a soda shop," she said with a wink. "Nothing is ever *that* wholesome."

"You're probably right." He took a seat on the couch and nodded for her to join him. "I assume you brought the paperwork?"

"I did, though now I'm thinking I should have just emailed them," she said as she glanced at the door. "I wouldn't have wasted so much of your time."

He shook his head. "You're never wasting my time. I'd much rather be sitting here with you than downstairs with the woman who showed up on my doorstep this morning unannounced. The one who after over thirty years suddenly wants to play my mother. The one who thinks making Christmas cookies will help us *bond*." The word was like sawdust on his tongue. "To tell you the truth, I didn't even know she knew how to make any cookies, much less Christmas ones."

Felicity blinked at him, her expression slightly startled. "I know you said your mother left when you were young, but did you really have no relationship with her at all?"

"No relationship," he confirmed. "She left me with my father and Tilly while she went off to pursue an acting and modeling career. She didn't show up again until after my father died. And only once a few years ago. It... didn't go well."

"What is she doing here now?" Felicity reached out and placed her hand on his chest. "Do you know?"

"No." He covered her hand with his. "And I'm doing everything I can to avoid finding out."

"Is that why we're up here?" she asked, giving him a cheeky smile.

"Yes." There was no point lying about it. "But also, I don't want her knowing your business. She doesn't have the greatest track record for discretion. I'd hate for you and your orchard to become a victim of the gossip mill."

"Surely she's not interested in my financial issues," Felicity said as she leaned back into the couch. "Why would she talk about that?"

"Why does Eva do anything she does? For attention, I suppose." He closed his eyes as he sucked in a deep breath, trying his best to clear the toxic energy from his mind and body. "But enough about that. Let me see your paperwork."

She opened the tote bag she was carrying and pulled out

a manila envelope. "This has both the foreclosure notice and a copy of the lien on the property."

Jackson tugged the paperwork out of the envelope and scanned them both. They certainly looked legit to him as well. The original lien was dated so far back he couldn't imagine it was a scam. Back in those days, Christmas Grove had been much smaller. Everyone knew their neighbors, and it would have been nearly impossible to place a lien without everyone knowing about it. The foreclosure was standard paperwork, but it had what he needed to track down who owned the LLC. "This will definitely get me started," he said. "I'm going to need to spend some time on the internet combing through records. You're welcome to stay if you want to. If not, I'll come out to the orchard and let you know what I find out."

"I wish I could stay," she said, giving him a tiny frown. "Unfortunately, I need to get back to work. We're almost out of Christmas Cheer."

Jackson jerked his head up to give her his full attention. "You're almost out? What happened? Did we use it all up last night?"

Felicity laughed, her eyes twinkling with amusement as she shook her head at him. "No, we didn't use it all up last night. I'm not talking about that anyway. Marilyn has enough of that kind of cheer to power the entire town of Christmas Grove for years to come. I mean Christmas Cheer, the apple-spiced drink we sell that is literally infused with some Christmas magic."

"And who makes that, Marilyn?" he guessed. "Do you run the store while she works her magic?"

"No." Felicity rolled her eyes at him. "*I* make it. I'm an earth witch with some unusual manifestations. As long as I use water from our spring, I'm able to charm the drink and infuse it with the ability to boost someone's mood significantly during the holiday season."

"So that's where all your Christmas joy ends up. In a drink that probably makes Christmas Grove residents downright giddy since most of them live for December." It was their favorite month after all. The excitement in the air was palpable at the end of November as the holiday approached. It only ratcheted up throughout the season as more and more magic filled the air.

"Ha. Ha. Very funny," Felicity said. Then she frowned. "Do you really think it's possible that's been part of my issue all along?"

"It could be," he said, "But I haven't seen what magic you put into this drink on a regular basis."

"Not much if I'm being honest. I mostly just activate the magic from the spring." She bit down on her bottom lip before she looked at Jackson and said, "No. I haven't had one spark of interest in Christmas since my grandmother died... until last night. So I definitely don't think I've been giving my joy away. I just don't have much to spare."

He hated that he knew she was speaking the truth. But he vowed to find more ways to bring her love for Christmas back. "Do you ice skate?"

She tilted her head. "Why?"

"It could be fun to go see if we can skate with the snowmen. Or if that's too adventurous for you, we could go up to the lodge at the ski resort and skate on their ice rink. The views are spectacular."

"Don't think I didn't see what you did there," she said. "If I agree to go, it's not a date."

"Of course not," he agreed, having already realized she wouldn't agree to that, even if he was going to treat it like one.

"And only after we've made significant progress on tracking down who's behind this loan/lien situation," she added.

"I wouldn't suggest otherwise," he said.

"Okay, good. As long as we're clear."

He loved it when Felicity got a little prickly. The challenge of coaxing her out of her comfort zone had proved to be more fun than he'd imagined. "We're clear."

"Well then. I should go," she said.

"I'll walk you out." He placed a hand on the small of her back and reveled in the fact that she didn't pull away.

Just as they were walking out of the sunroom, Eva appeared with a plate of cookies. "Oh, you're leaving already? I brought you a snack."

"Eva—" Jackson started, but Felicity cut him off.

"That was kind of you," Felicity said, her voice sugar sweet. "But I've already gotten the sugar I came for." She winked at Jackson. "See you later, honey. My place? Seven tonight?"

He could have kissed her right then and there. It was his

night off at Sleighed and Felicity Hill had just given him an out for the evening. "Seven it is."

"Don't be late. You're cooking," she called over her shoulder.

All Jackson could do was laugh.

"What's so funny, sweetheart?" Eva asked.

It was all he could do to keep from scowling at her. How dare she call him sweetheart? That was far too familiar for a mother who'd barely been in his life for five minutes. "Inside joke." He glanced down at the cookies on the tray. The edges were burned and the middles looked soft. He couldn't resist saying, "Your oven temperature is too high. Turn it down about fifty degrees next time and bake them a few minutes longer."

"Oh. Okay." Her hopeful expression had vanished and turned into one of defeat. "I'll just go downstairs and clean up."

He didn't say anything else, knowing he was being a jerk, but he just couldn't make himself pretend he was happy she was there. Especially when she was using up all his ingredients on burned, underbaked cookies.

When Eva was gone, Jackson grabbed Felicity's paperwork and took a seat at his desk, ready to do some investigating.

Hours later, with his eyes crossing from his internet sleuthing, Jackson finally shut his laptop and hopped into the shower. When he was clean, freshly shaved, and dressed, he went downstairs and looked for his mother. He found her curled up in a chair near the fireplace, her head buried in her phone.

"You're going out?" she asked, startled to see him.

"Yes. Do you have everything you need?" It was the first time his manners had kicked in since she'd arrived.

"I'm fine. When will you be back?"

Even though he knew he was being ridiculous, he felt like a teenager being grilled before heading out on a date. He just shrugged. "I'm not sure." Then he turned and reached for the doorknob.

Before he could escape, his mother said, "Well, have fun. Don't forget the condoms."

He jerked his head, turning in her direction.

"You know what they say, 'no glove, no love.'" Then she laughed.

"Right." He gave her a nod and then left, feeling a huge weight lift off him the moment he stepped off his front porch.

CHAPTER 9

"So, you're dating Jackson Bell now?" Clara asked as she sipped wine from her favorite chair in their sunroom.

Felicity gave her annoying friend a flat stare. "You know I don't date the marrying kind."

"Oh?" Clara brushed back a lock of her raven-colored hair and smirked when she said, "Then I guess you won't mind if I ask him out?"

A lightning bolt of irritation shot through Felicity's limbs, and she gritted her teeth as she said, "If that's what you want to do. I know he's exactly your type."

Clara threw her head back and cackled. "If only you could see the look on your face. Are you really sitting there telling me that you wouldn't want to murder me in my sleep if I started dating Jackson?"

"I didn't say that," Felicity said, leaning back into the love seat. "But who am I to stand in the way of two people finding love and their happily-ever-after."

"You're full of crap." Clara plucked a piece of cheese off the plate sitting on the end table next to her and popped it into her mouth. "And you know damned well I'd never go after one of your men, even if you are determined to sleep with every bachelor under the age of forty." She grinned at Felicity.

"Don't slut shame," Felicity said haughtily, even though she knew Clara was only joking. The truth was, that while Felicity talked a good game and enjoyed a night out with a fun date every now and then, she rarely hooked up with anyone. Maybe she was picky, but she just hadn't found anyone worth the trouble. Or she hadn't until Jackson Bell had come along.

Clara raised the bottle of wine, offering it to her friend.

"I think I'm going to go for coffee instead." Felicity got to her feet. "Need anything while I'm in the kitchen?"

"The number of a hot man who's looking for a serious girlfriend, please," Clara said. "And a hex for that loser Peter, who turned out to be dating three of us at the same time."

"Gladly. One that will shrivel little Peter and make it burn when he pees," Felicity said, still fuming over the seemingly sweet guy who'd taken glass blowing classes from Clara over the spring and then wined and dined her through the fall. She'd thought they were getting serious and had been over the moon when she'd accidently stumbled upon tickets for a Hawaiian vacation for two. She'd thought it was going to be a surprise for her birthday.

It was a surprise all right. But it wasn't a trip to Hawaii for her. It was for another girlfriend he'd been dating for three years who lived down in the Bay Area. When all was finally out in the open, Clara had learned Peter currently was dating her, the woman in the Bay Area, and another up in Lake Tahoe. He traveled for work all over the northern part of the state, and that was how he'd managed to juggle everyone at the same time.

She'd really liked him, and he'd broken her heart. But worse, he'd caused her to lose some of that eternal optimism that made her Clara. And for that, Felicity would gladly hex him into oblivion. Too bad she wasn't that kind of witch. Her magic was focused on healing and joy, not revenge.

Hopefully Peter would run into a vindictive witch someday soon. It was what he deserved.

Felicity had just doctored her coffee when the doorbell rang. "Jingle Bells" started to play, and she groaned. "Clara! Seriously?"

"It's festive!" her friend called back.

"Why couldn't you have chosen Vince Guaraldi instead? At least that's tolerable."

"Because the Charlie Brown Christmas music is the only music you let me play normally. I wanted something *fun*. Live with it."

"Fine," Felicity shot back. She knew she could be a Grinch, but they played all the holiday favorites at Apples and Spice and Everything Nice all day. A girl could only take so much.

"I knew you'd see it my way."

Chuckling, Felicity opened the door to find the very handsome Jackson Bell standing on her doorstep, looking like an angel with a bag of groceries. "Jackson Bell, are you really cooking for me and Clara tonight? I made that comment for your mom's benefit."

"That's the plan. As long as you both like mushroom risotto."

"Risotto? Oh. Em. Gee. Let the man in, Felicity," Clara said as she rushed to push her friend out of the way. "Come in, come in," she added as she held the door open wider, giving him space.

Felicity rolled her eyes and muttered, "Hands off the man candy."

"You said you wouldn't mind if I dated him," she muttered back.

"What was that?" Jackson asked as he glanced back at them, frowning.

"Nothing," they both said at once.

Felicity fell into step behind Jackson and couldn't help admiring him. He looked amazing in his tight jeans and fitted sweater, and he smelled of something woodsy that made her warm all over. Or was that the way his butt filled out his jeans?

Maybe both.

"Want some wine, Jackson?" Clara asked once they made it into the kitchen.

"Not just yet," he said, already making himself at home as he unpacked his groceries. "But definitely with dinner."

"All right." She glanced between Felicity and Jackson before grinning like a fool when she said, "I'm gonna go do some work on my computer and give you kids some time to chat. Call me if you need help with anything."

"You don't need to go," Felicity called after her friend, but Clara just raised a hand in the air and hurried off to her bedroom.

"That was subtle," Jackson said with a chuckle.

"She's a dreamer," Felicity said as she took a seat at the bar, still holding her coffee mug. "Clara thinks that taunting me with asking you out is going to make me want to lock you down."

"Is she right?" he asked, his lips twitching with amusement.

Yes. "No. I'm not the commitment type," she said for what felt like the hundredth time. But the words rang hollow, and she frowned, wondering where that feeling had come from. She quickly pushed the thought aside and changed the subject. "Were you able to find anything out about the person behind the foreclosure?"

Jackson pressed his lips together and shook his head. "Not yet. I did order the LLC paperwork. The company has a registered agent listed as the owner, which means I haven't been able to track down who exactly is behind the foreclosure yet. My next step is to go down to the assessor's office to check the archives on your property. The LLC associated with the lien is relatively new. That means the lien has been updated. The archives should be a treasure trove of information."

"I want to go with you," Felicity said. "When do you have time? Tomorrow?"

He nodded. "I can be there right when they open. How about you, can you take time away from your shop?"

"For something this important? Yes," she said. Marilyn would just have to handle the morning rush without her. If they didn't figure out what to do about the loan, there wouldn't be an Apples and Spice and Everything Nice in just a few short weeks.

"It's a date then," he said.

"A date?" Clara echoed as she walked back into the kitchen. "Are you taking her to the Christmas ball, Jackson?"

"The Christmas ball?" he asked. "What's that?"

The petite woman clapped her hands together as she bounced on her toes. "It's a fundraiser for underprivileged kids. Everyone is supposed to dress in their holiday best and dance the night away under an enchanted moon. It's next Friday night. You can get tickets at the Frost Family Tree Farm. The Frosts are sponsoring it this year."

"That sounds very festive," Jackson said. "What do you say, Felicity? Will you let me spin you around the dance floor for an evening?"

"I don't—" she started.

"It's for charity, Felicity," Clara said, giving her a stern look. "You're going one way or another. You can either be Jackson's date or be the third wheel on mine."

"Who are you going with?" Felicity demanded.

"That's a surprise." She gave her friend a cheeky grin, and Felicity suspected that Clara didn't have a date at all.

"You're a pain in my butt, you know that?" Felicity said to Clara. Then because she secretly really did want to go to the ball with Jackson she said, "Yes, I'd much rather go with you than be a third wheel with Clara and Old Man Percy at the Christmas ball."

Clara burst out laughing. Percy was the old farmer who was in a hometown rock band. He often hung out at Sleighed when they weren't playing and told stories of what Christmas Grove used to be like when he was a younger man. He had tales of saloons and brothels, including one that started selling enchanted glass ornaments. He was forever telling Clara that she needed to get in on that market even though she already did.

"Now he might be a fun date," Clara said, shaking her head. "But only if I wanted to hear all about his first 'experience' with one of the madams at the Naughty and Nice Gentleman's club."

Felicity snickered. "You might learn a few things."

"Maybe so," Clara agreed.

Jackson cleared his throat. "Do I want to know about the Naughty and Nice club? It sounds like a roadside girly bar one might find on Interstate 5 outside of Sacramento."

"Oh no. It was a brothel right here in Christmas Grove. It's actually, in its own weird way, how this town ended up being built up around Christmas," Felicity said. "They sold enchanted glass ornaments, and the men would buy them for their significant others when they were passing through. From there, other Christmas-related businesses built up, and now here we are."

"You're kidding," he said.

"That's what Old Man Percy says," Clara said.

"My grandmother said it didn't quite happen like that," Felicity added, "But I think she might have been trying to spare my delicate ears."

"Well, that certainly adds a little flavor to Christmas Grove now, doesn't it?" Jackson said, clearly amused.

"It does," Both Felicity and Clara said at the same time.

"Now, how can I help?" Clara asked as she moved into the kitchen.

Jackson had her stand by the stove to keep stirring the risotto while Felicity set the table. By the time dinner was ready to be served, the entire house was filled with an aroma that made her stomach growl.

"Someone is hungry," Clara said. "Should have joined me when I had that snack earlier."

"No way. Now I have room for more," she said as she took her seat next to Jackson. "Do you take on private clients? I think Clara and I might want to hire you as our personal chef."

"Sorry," he said, shaking his head. But then he put on a teasing smile as he added, "I'm not for hire. However, I am persuadable."

"Persuade him!" Clara said with a mouthful of risotto. Her eyes rolled into the back of her head as she swallowed the yummy goodness. "You're a god."

Felicity glanced at Jackson.

He raised one eyebrow. "Did you hear that? I'm a god. What more could you want in a man?"

The ridiculously handsome man cooked. He helped plow roads. And he was trying his best to help her save her orchard. Honestly, Felicity had no idea what more she could possibly need.

CHAPTER 10

*A*fter dinner, Clara insisted that she'd clean up while Jackson and Felicity relaxed by the fire. Jackson was ready to take her up on the offer, but Felicity dead refused.

"No way. I not a lady of leisure," Felicity said. "I'll help, then we can *all* go relax with the rest of this wine."

Clara gave Jackson a look that said she'd tried and then went back to the dishes.

"Go on," Felicity said to him. "We won't be long. Find a movie or something on the television."

"Something Christmasy," Clara called. "We have the Hallmark channel."

"No Hallmark!" Felicity said.

"Ah-ha!" Clara pointed at her. "You didn't rule out Christmas entirely. Jackson, hurry and find some holiday movie on Netflix. It's time for some Christmas cheer up in this joint."

He laughed at them and then disappeared into the living room with his glass of wine. After settling on the couch, he picked up the remote, intending to look for one of the classics. But instead, as soon as the television came on, he found himself staring at his mother, Eva.

She was dressed in a red velvet dress, had her long blond hair piled up in an elaborate bun, and was wearing white furry gloves as she clutched a microphone and said, "Thanks for having me, Bert."

Bert was the local television host who ran segments about what was happening in Christmas Grove every day during the holiday season. Marissa kept it on at Sleighed so that the patrons could learn about any happenings around town.

The event that night was a holiday art fair down at the square. There were booths set up behind his mother as patrons strolled from tent to tent, looking for the perfect holiday gifts.

"What are you going to sing for us tonight? Bert asked her.

"Sing?" she asked, her face flushing as if she were shy. "I didn't plan anything. This was so last minute…" She trailed off and then said, "I guess I'll do 'Baby it's Cold Outside.'"

"Wonderful! Wonderful!" Bert said. "Well folks, it looks like we're in for a special treat as Eva Bell, the star from the fan favorite show *Harmony Heights,* just happens to be visiting Christmas Grove for the season. Without further ado, take it away, Eva!"

His mother shifter her glance down, and then when she

started the first note, she looked up at the camera through her fake eyelashes as if she were flirting with the audience.

"Oh wow, is that your mother?" Felicity said, startling him out of his trance. "I didn't know she was performing tonight."

"Neither did I," he said, still watching her belt out the song.

"That's your mom?" Clara practically shouted as she climbed into a chair and crossed her legs. "She has a nice voice."

"She was on that family singing show like twenty years ago," Felicity said. "Do you remember it? She was the stage mom who was always trying to protect the kids from the industry."

Jackson snorted.

"You didn't like it?" Clara asked him.

"No." How could he? His mom had left him and then spent half a decade playing an overprotective mom who always put her kids first. She deserved an Emmy for that role. "It just wasn't my thing."

The three of them watched in silence as Eva played up the song. When she finally ended the last note, she looked flushed and shy as if she wasn't sure she should even be there, playing up the role of doing the host a favor.

Jackson stared at her clutching the microphone as she turned her profile to the camera, making sure she was giving a good angle, and he felt the cold calculation radiating from her as his empath gift kicked in full force. It was unusual for him to feel emotions from someone on a television set, but it wasn't unheard of. His gift was random and extremely unpredictable. It wasn't as if he could just call up his gift and read someone's emotions anytime he wanted to. The best he could figure out over the years was that his gift kicked in when he was *supposed* to feel someone's emotions for a specific reason. Usually either so he could help them or so that he could be warned.

This was clearly a warning. It wasn't an accident that his mother was at the holiday fair. That much was obvious from the way she'd dressed as if she were a snow queen. She'd gone down to the square hoping for this exact scenario.

But why? No one from Hollywood was going to be watching the news in Christmas Grove and remember that Eva Bell used to be a slightly famous actress who could hold a tune and then miraculously hire her as the star in some film.

"Oh, look!" Clara said, pointing at the screen as the cameraman panned the square. "Looks like they're setting up to film another holiday movie."

Jackson narrowed his eyes as he studied the television. Over the years, Christmas Grove had become a hot spot for filming Christmas movies during December when the town was in full season. This year was no exception.

With that realization, a vision of his mother in her red velvet dress literally running into the director flashed in his mind. He saw his mother bat her fake eyelashes at him as she clutched his arm and apologized for not looking where she was going. In the vision, he saw them walk off, their heads bent together as she grasped his arm.

He sucked in a long breath, finally understanding why his mother was in Christmas Grove. She was trying to create a relationship with the director so that she could find some work. His heart ached a little, and he silently berated himself for it. He'd known all along that there must have been some sort of ulterior motive for Eva showing up on his doorstep. It just pained him to be proven right.

"How was your evening?" Eva asked from her spot on the couch in front of the television when Jackson finally walked back into his house just after midnight. She was fresh-faced, no sign of makeup, and her hair had been plaited into a side braid. Her feet were ensconced in fluffy slippers that matched her robe, and everything about her screamed that she'd spent a quiet night in watching Hallmark movies.

"It was good," he said, trying for a cheerful tone. He wanted to see if she was going to tell him about her night out or if she'd just pretend she'd spent the night alone on the couch. "How was yours?"

"Quiet." She smiled and then nodded at the television. "I spent it getting caught up on the latest Christmas movies. You know I'm always so busy down in LA that I barely have time to watch anything." She picked up the remote and clicked the TV off. "But it's late now, so I'd better get to bed."

Jackson nodded, wondering why she felt the need to lie to him. What was she trying to get out of him that she couldn't just tell the truth?

She rose gracefully from the couch, walked over to him, and pressed her hand to one cheek as she kissed the other. "I sure would like to spend some time with you tomorrow, baby. Do you think you could spare some time for your sweet old mom?"

His jaw twitched with the effort to keep from snapping at her. She was a decent actress, but he saw right through her facade. Her nervous energy combined with that coldness he'd felt earlier made him want to take a step back. To tell her to pack her bags and leave. But something inside of him just wouldn't let him kick her out. He didn't know why. She didn't deserve anything from him.

Maybe it was that little boy who'd always wished his mother would come home.

Or maybe it was morbid curiosity.

He didn't know. Either way, he shook his head and said, "Sorry. I have plans with Felicity tomorrow."

"Can't you reschedule?" she asked, trying for hopeful, but he felt the desperation underneath. "I just want to get brunch and—"

"No. It's important. We can do brunch another day."

Eva frowned, her lips barely curving down, and Jackson couldn't help wondering just how much plastic surgery she'd had to make her face so taut and unmovable. "Fine," she said with a sigh. "I'll just have to go to brunch by myself."

She was annoyed. He didn't care.

"Goodnight, Eva," he said.

"I wish you'd just call me mom like you used to as a little boy," she said. This time there wasn't anything calculating about her. She meant what she said. But the fact that there was zero guilt mixed in with the emotions radiating off her made Jackson's blood boil.

"It's too late for that, Eva," he said. "Goodnight." Then he took off up the stairs, leaving her standing there staring after him.

CHAPTER 11

"Good morning," Felicity said as Jackson climbed out of his truck holding a pink pastry box. "Please tell me there's a maple bar in that box with my name on it."

"What will you give me for it?" he asked as his lips curved up into a whisper of a smile.

"Coffee?" She waved at the to-go tray that was sitting in her passenger seat.

"Seriously? You truly are a goddess." He opened the box, revealing a maple bar and two glazed donuts.

"And you sir, are my hero," she said, trading a coffee for a pastry.

It was just before nine, and they were standing in front of the county assessor's office, waiting for them to open. A few snow flurries swirled around them in the gentle breeze, and after finishing her pastry, Felicity looked up at the sky, wondering if they were in for another storm. And if so, how could she get Jackson back to her orchard for another night at the cabin? Her gaze landed on the man in question, who was wearing a fitted sweater and jeans that did amazing things for his backside.

"Felicity?" he asked.

She jerked her attention away from his chest and formfitting sweater to meet his eyes. "Huh?"

"The clerk is here. Are you ready to go in?" There was a knowing smile on his lips, and she had no doubt she'd been caught ogling him.

"Of course. Lead the way," she said, ignoring the fact that her cheeks were flushing with heat.

"It's not often I get company this early in the morning," the clerk said as she tucked a runaway, bottle-dyed red curl behind her ear. She wore glasses with a beaded chain around her neck and looked like she'd been a permanent fixture at the office for the last fifty years or so. "What can I help you with today?"

Felicity explained she was looking for lien documents that had been filed against her property. "I just need to find the originals so that I can track down exactly who my grandmother borrowed money from."

"Normally that wouldn't be too big of a problem," the clerk said with a slight frown. "But we just moved offices a few weeks ago, and not everything is organized yet. We don't have all the boxes from the old storage unit moved in, but everything should be in the database."

"We'll start with the database," Jackson said. "Then we'll see what physical copies we might need."

"Sure thing. Help yourself to the computers," the clerk said. "Let me know if you need any help."

"Thank you..." Felicity looked around, searching for a name plate. When she found it, she smiled. "Thank you, Doris."

"You're very welcome. I hope you find what you're looking for."

"Me too," Felicity said under her breath as she followed Jackson to the old computer that had to be circa 1990s. It was a large cream-colored beast that looked like it belonged in the Smithsonian, not the town assessor's office.

Jackson pressed the button on the monitor, making the machine beep just before the Windows 95 logo filled the screen.

"This is what they use for organizing their files?" Felicity asked, wondering if she should start a collection plate to upgrade the town's computer.

"At least it isn't a microfiche reader," Jackson said. "You have no idea how many small towns are still using those for looking up old records."

Felicity blinked at him. "Microfiche? Seriously?"

"Yep. Talk about the dark ages." He tapped the Enter key on the computer, making a text box appear. Then he entered the address of her orchard. After a long moment, a bunch of numbers started to populate the screen. He clicked the first one, and the property details for Apples and Spice and Everything Nice popped up, showing that the property taxes had been paid. He clicked another one and found a survey record. The next set of numbers wasn't linked to anything. When Jackson clicked on it, nothing happened.

"Doris?" Felicity called as she walked toward the counter. "What does it mean when a record isn't linked to anything?"

"Oh, honey. That just means the record hasn't been scanned in yet," Doris said, already walking toward them. "You're going to need to dig through the files."

Felicity glanced around the room, taking in the stacks of banker boxes. Each one was labeled with a set of numbers. "We need to dig through these?"

"Yes," Doris said with a nod. She peered over Jackson's shoulder at the numbered file. Then she quickly wrote it down and walked around the room until she stopped at a stack of boxes. "See this number?" She pointed to her paper and then a box that was on the bottom. "See how the first three numbers match? That's how you'll find the box you're looking for."

"We've got it," Jackson said. He nodded toward the computer screen. "Can I print these out?"

"Sure thing. Just hit Control P." Doris grinned at him, looking pleased with herself as if she'd just helped him solve some secret code.

The printer came to life and made an ungodly amount of noise as it printed out the numbers of the files Jackson hadn't been able to open.

"I'll be at the desk if you need me," Doris said cheerily.

"Good to know," Felicity muttered as she eyed the dusty banker boxes. She'd imagined that they'd check the computer, find what they needed, and she'd already be making a plan to go see whoever held the lien on her property. Instead, she was getting ready to move heavy boxes and would no doubt be sneezing up a storm as soon as they disturbed the many layers of dust.

"Here," Jackson said, handing her a sheet of paper that had half the numbers circled. "You look for these. I'll do the other half. With any luck, we'll be out of here before lunch."

Felicity grimaced, sent a text to Marilyn letting her know she'd be a little later than planned, and then got to work, looking for the paperwork. The first two files she found were for permits. One was to update the cabin's plumbing, and the other was for a septic repair. She crossed them off her list and pushed her hair out of her eyes as she went for the next box.

Three files later, she sat heavily on one of the plastic chairs and blew out a frustrated breath. "I don't see anything about a lien."

"I don't either. Not yet anyway," Jackson said as he looked up and let out a small chuckle.

"Something funny?" she asked, more than a little bit annoyed.

"Just that smudge of dirt on your nose." He winked at her as he pulled the lid off another box.

"Great." She rose and went to find the small restroom. After cleaning herself up, she returned to the records room and frowned when she spotted Jackson standing in the middle of the room scowling. "What's wrong?"

"There are a few boxes missing." He waved his paper at her. "These last two numbers are nowhere to be found."

"Try that storage closet!" Doris yelled from across the room.

They both turned and looked at the closed door.

Felicity shrugged and went to inspect the closet. When she opened the door, something flew out at her, causing her to let out a cry as she raised her hands and ducked at the same time. "Oh, my sweet Santa! What in the Christmas nightmare was that?"

"Looked like a moth," Jackson said.

"No way. That thing was the size of my head!" She peered into the dark closet, wary of being attacked.

Jackson let out a soft chuckle. "It wasn't that big. Here. There's a light." He reached in and flicked the switch.

Soft lighting illuminated a full closet of boxes.

None of them were labeled.

They both groaned.

Felicity retreated to go find Doris.

"Yes, dear? Did you need help?" the woman asked as she looked up from her paperwork.

"None of the boxes in the closet are labeled. Are you sure we're supposed to be searching in there?" Felicity asked.

Doris gave her an apologetic smile. "Yes. The first girl we had helping us pack up was… Well, being detail oriented wasn't her strong suit. She got all of those done before anyone noticed she wasn't documenting them. You'll just have to open them and see what's stored there."

Felicity ground her teeth together and forced out, "Thanks."

"No problem!" Doris waved cheerily, clearly happy to have company on the cold morning.

Felicity walked back to Jackson, who was leaning against the closet door. "Let's do this," she said. "One box at a time."

He shook his head. "I was afraid of that." Taking a deep breath, he started pulling boxes out into the room.

They quickly got to work.

Two hours later, Felicity sat on the dusty floor with boxes surrounding her, ready to pull her hair out. "These files just aren't here!"

Jackson closed the box he'd been searching and frowned. "Maybe we missed some?"

"No, that's it," Doris said, appearing right beside Jackson. "If you're still missing some files, they are probably still in storage."

"There are more files in storage?" Felicity blurted, ready to throttle Doris and her perky attitude. "Please tell me those are labeled."

"Oh, they are. They just aren't here," she said with a frown.

"Where are they?" Felicity demanded.

"We're still in the process of bringing everything over, so they're still at the old building."

"Is anyone there?" Jackson asked. "Will they let us in if we go over there?"

"Oh no," Doris said with a nervous giggle. "It's just me, and I can't be in two places at once now, can I?"

Felicity was ready to scream, but she swallowed the impulse. "Miss Doris, it's very important that I find these documents as soon as possible. When do you think the records will be available?"

"You just leave those numbers with me and I'll find them for you," she said, holding her hand out.

"You are a godsend," Felicity said, handing her the now-crumpled piece of paper. "When can I expect your call? Tomorrow?"

"Tomorrow?" Doris asked, looking surprised. "Oh no. I won't be able to go through those files until next Friday when I go over to the other building with my son to start bringing more boxes over here."

"We can't wait that long," Felicity said, alarmed. "It's Monday now. Waiting all week just isn't possible. Is there any way we can get to those files sooner? My property is on the line."

"Oh." Doris bit down on her bottom lip. "I suppose I could go by in the morning and take a look."

"Perfect," Felicity said, reaching out and giving the woman a hug. "You are a Christmas angel."

"An angel? I don't know about that," Doris said with a tiny laugh as she took a step back. Her lips were curved into a smile, and a sparkle shone from her bright green eyes.

"I think she's right," Jackson said, giving Doris a hug of his own. "Thank you for your help."

"Of course." Doris stepped back and stared down at her pink blazer. Frowning, she used both hands to wipe off the dust that Jackson had transferred to her jacket. Then the phone rang and she hurried back to her desk.

Felicity looked at Jackson. "I guess that's it for today?"

"I'm sorry it wasn't more successful," he said, placing his hand on the small of her back. "Hopefully Doris comes through for us."

"From your lips to the goddess's ears."

Once they were outside, Jackson walked her to her Jeep. "Will I see you tonight at Sleighed?"

"That depends," she said, eyeing him.

"On?"

"If you're specifically asking me to come by." Felicity felt a flutter in her gut, the one that usually sent her running in the other direction. But for some reason, all she wanted to hear was that Jackson wanted to see her.

"I am. I was hoping for a drink after I get off work. What do you say?" He held her gaze, his piercing dark eyes making her want things she'd long ago decided weren't for her.

"Just one drink," she said, already knowing that one drink would never be enough.

Jackson reached out and brushed his thumb over her cheekbone. Then he leaned in and brushed his lips over her skin. "I'll be waiting."

Felicity watched as he climbed into his truck, unable to tear her gaze from his perfect backside. Finally, when he was settled in his vehicle, she climbed into her Jeep and then followed him out of the still-deserted parking lot.

CHAPTER 12

ackson was in desperate need of a shower. After moving all the boxes at the assessor's office, dirt seemed to cover every inch of him, and his eyes were burning from the dust mites. He pulled up next to a silver Escalade that was parked in his driveway and frowned. His mother's Ford Escort rental was still parked where she'd left it, which meant that one of them had company.

He stepped out of his truck and did a double take when he spotted his front porch. In addition to the garland and wreath he'd hung a week earlier, there was now a fully decorated Christmas tree off to the side, fake frost on the window, and Santa and Mrs. Claus garden gnomes to the left of the door. "What in the world?" he wondered to himself.

Where had that stuff come from, and more importantly, why did his mother feel it was okay to redecorate his home?

Dreading the confrontation, he walked into the house and came to a dead stop when the overwhelming scent of cinnamon hit him just as he spotted his mother climbing off the lap of a silver-haired man whose suit jacket was pushed off his shoulders, and his white button-down shirt was partially unbuttoned.

Jackson blinked at them, grateful that they were both still fully clothed even if they were a little rumpled from their make-out session.

The man quickly stood, and Jackson recognized him as the director his mother had been trying to cozy up to in the vision he'd had the night before. His stomach turned as he realized exactly what he'd just walked in on.

"Jackson," his mother said with a nervous laugh. "I didn't think you'd be home until later tonight after you got off work."

He turned to stare at his mother, making a concerted effort to not grimace at her appearance. Her red lipstick was smeared, and her hair was mussed. "I don't work until later this afternoon."

"Hello, Jackson," the man said as he held out his hand. "I've been anxious to meet you... though not quite under these circumstances." He flashed a rueful smile. "You have such a lovely home. It's going to be perfect for this movie we're filming."

"Movie?" Jackson blinked at him, ignoring his outstretched hand. "What movie?"

"The one I'm starring in, honey," Eva said as she grabbed

Jackson's arm and squeezed just hard enough to indicate she meant business. "I told you about it last night," she lied.

Jackson narrowed his eyes at his mother, but before he could question her, she continued.

"Larry has been kind enough to cast me as the Christmas Queen in his upcoming movie, and when he mentioned they needed a quaint farmhouse for the filming, I mentioned your place, and he loves it. It's going to look fabulous on screen."

"You want to use my house to film?" Jackson asked, ready to tell them both to take a hike. He wasn't interested in having a bunch of strangers romping around his property.

"Of course they do," Eva said, smiling at Larry.

Larry frowned at her. "I thought you said your son was already on board with this, Eva. You said it was a done deal. My crew already stopped looking for filming locations, and being that we're supposed to start tomorrow, if that's not the case, then I'm not sure the project can go forward at all."

Panic flashed in Eva's sky-blue eyes. "Don't worry, Larry. I think there's just been a slight misunderstanding." She tugged on Jackson's arm as she started to head toward the kitchen. "Give us just a minute, and we'll have this all worked out. Wait here. We'll be right back."

"I've got contracts that need to be signed today, Eva," Larry called after her. "And I don't have all day."

Jackson cast a side-eye glance at the man, disgust pooling at the back of his throat. Larry sure hadn't seemed in a hurry when Eva had been straddling him a few minutes ago.

Eva walked through the kitchen and led Jackson out onto the back deck. Once the door was firmly closed, she said, "Jackson, please. I need this."

"Need what? To sleep with the director so that you can get a part in a movie? How cliché of you." He was furious and couldn't find it in himself to temper his words.

"What? No. I already have the part. The contract is signed," she said indignantly. "I'm an adult woman, and how I choose to spend my time and who with isn't really any of your business."

"It is when you're doing it on my couch," he shot back. "And when you're promising my house for a film without ever even asking me about it. When was I going to find out? When they were setting up for filming?"

"No." She glanced away, focusing on one of the large trees. "I was going to ask you last night, but then you were out and you left earlier than I expected this morning. Then Larry came over to get the contracts signed—"

"Larry brought the contracts? Isn't that something a production assistant does?" he asked. "Aren't most contracts sent through Docusign these days? It seems Larry wanted a lot more than just a signature."

"Obviously we have more than just a working relationship," Eva snapped. "That's not what this is about."

"Isn't it?" he asked as he crossed his arms over his chest and glared at her. "Regardless, the answer is no. I'm not giving up my house and my space for some movie. Haven't you figured out why I moved to Christmas Grove in the first place? It was for peace and quiet. Why would I want movie people crawling around my home?"

She matched his stance with her arms crossed. "You haven't even heard what they are willing to pay you."

"I. Don't. Care." He stared her down.

"You will when you see the check," she shot back.

That's where she was dead wrong. Jackson didn't need the money. He'd made enough in his previous career to set up a decent retirement, and when he'd sold his fancy penthouse condo to move to Christmas Grove, he'd paid cash for his house. His job at Sleighed was more than enough to keep his bills paid with plenty left over for ski trips and home maintenance and any other thing he needed. He started to shake his head, but then the image of Felicity searching through all that paperwork earlier flashed in his mind. What if the money from the filming could help her with that lien? He'd happily hand it over if it meant her land wasn't yanked out from underneath her due to something she had no control over. Though he had serious doubts she'd accept it.

"If you don't allow them to film, then they likely won't film at all," Eva said in a small voice. "I didn't want to say anything because it's embarrassing, but if I don't work, I won't get paid, and then I'll be evicted from my apartment in LA. Times are tight, Jackson. I need this. If the movie does well, there's a good chance Larry will cast me for more of his feel-good movies, and I'll be able to stand on my own two feet again. If not, I'm afraid I might have to beg you to let me move in here."

There was so much to unpack from her plea that Jackson wasn't even sure where to start. He'd almost shut her down the minute she'd said she might become a regular in Larry's movies. Since he filmed a lot in Christmas Grove, it meant Eva would be around more often. Not something he wanted to encourage. However, if she was serious and she really was on the verge of being homeless, he had no doubt that she'd beg to stay with him, which was a hard no. He could not have Eva living with him full time. One of them wouldn't survive it. The threat of her moving in, along with the idea that he could have the extra money available to help Felicity, was enough for him to ask, "How much is the rental agreement?"

A brilliant smile appeared on her lips as she pulled out her phone and tapped a few buttons. "I just sent you a copy of the proposal. It's very generous. Larry is anxious to get moving on this, and he offered an amount that is very hard to turn down."

Jackson checked his email and pulled up the paperwork. The amount to use his house until just before Christmas had five zeros behind it. She was right. It was the kind of money that most people wouldn't turn down. "I'll have to read the contract first, but if they are out of here by Christmas Eve, then I think maybe we might have a deal."

She bit down on her bottom lip. "There's just one thing."

He ground his teeth together and waited.

"We'll both have to move out for the next few weeks."

Jackson blinked at her. "If you're on the verge of being homeless, where do you plan to stay?"

"In the trailer that production provides," she said, once again giving him an apologetic smile. "I'd invite you to stay there with me, but I can't. Only the crew is allowed on set where the trailers are."

There was no way in hell he'd stay with his mother in a small trailer anyway. "I'll figure something out." He turned and walked back into the house.

Larry was standing in the kitchen door. "Do we have a deal?"

"Let me read the contract first," Jackson said. "But as long as it's acceptable, I'll pack a bag and be out of your way by tonight."

"Good man!" Larry said, clasping him on the back. "You're a lifesaver. A lot of people are going to be very happy we don't have to shut down production."

Jackson wasn't born yesterday. He'd been a player in big business long enough to smell a bluff when an executive was full of crap, but that didn't matter. He had his own reasons for saying yes, and neither the director nor his mother needed to know that their manipulations hadn't been the major driving factor in his decision.

Once Jackson was upstairs in his office, he printed off the contract, read every word, and then signed it.

Ten minutes later, he walked downstairs with two bags and handed the signed contract to Larry. "Good luck with the movie. I'll be back on Christmas Eve. If the house isn't in the same or better condition, rest assured I will be in touch with my lawyers."

"Don't worry about that, Mr. Bell. My crew is the best. Check with other residents we've leased from, and they will assure you that we take pride in our work and making sure we'll be invited back next year."

Jackson just nodded at him and then strode out the front door.

His mother followed him out. "Jackson?"

"Yes," he said as he loaded his bags in his truck.

"Thank you."

He glanced back at her, noting that her expression seemed more sincere than it had before. Now that she'd gotten what she wanted, she truly was grateful. "You're welcome. I hope the movie turns things around for you."

"Me, too." She ran off the porch and threw her arms around him. "You're the best boy a mom could ask for."

Jackson awkwardly patted her back with one arm as she held on tight. It wasn't until he cleared his throat and dropped his arm that she finally took a step back.

Wiping at her eyes, she said, "Can we get together for lunch or dinner sometime this week?"

"Breakfast would be better," he said. "I can meet for coffee one morning. Text me with what day is good for you."

"Okay. I'll try," she said.

Not caring one way or another, he nodded and climbed

into his truck. As he drove away, he realized that renting his house out for film production also had the added benefit of putting space between him and his mother. That alone was almost enough to make it worth it.

CHAPTER 13

"Any luck?" Marilyn asked as Felicity walked into the store carrying a bag of sandwiches from town.

Felicity let out an exaggerated sigh. "No. The assessor's office is a hot mess. Doris, the clerk, is going to do some digging for us in the morning. Hopefully by then I'll know exactly who is behind this lien so I can figure out how to deal with it going forward."

"I still think it's a mistake," Marilyn said, the lines around her eyes deepening as she frowned. "Kitty was never one to ignore a debt. There is no way she'd saddle you with this."

Felicity nodded her agreement. "That's why I thought it was a scam at first. But the lawyer says it's legit, so here we are, forced to track down paperwork to see if we can get to the bottom of it."

"I wish there was something I could do to help." Marilyn

wiped the pie counter, even though the surface was already spotless. Tears filled her eyes as she added, "Kitty would be heartbroken to see you struggling with this."

Felicity's eyes burned, but she quickly blinked back the tears. "Enough of that, Marilyn. This is no time to be worrying about that. Jackson is helping me, and we're going to do everything in our power to make sure this orchard stays in the Hill family for decades to come."

The words sounded hollow to Felicity's own ears. Considering she was the last Hill, they both knew that eventually the orchard would be sold off since there was no heir.

Yet.

Not that Felicity planned on getting married and having kids. Maybe she'd leave the orchard to Clara's or Marissa's kids. That seemed plausible. But only if she managed to hang onto it long enough.

The phone rang.

Felicity grabbed it. "Apples and Spice and Everything Nice. How may I help you today?"

The person on the other end of the line cleared their throat. "Hi, this is Sherry Castle. I'm supposed to be renting your cabin for the next two weeks."

Supposed to be? Felicity thought immediately as dread started to coil in her gut. She took a deep breath, bracing for the worst. "Hi Sherry, this is Felicity. How can I help?"

"Well," the woman said, sounding tired. "We've had a family emergency, and my husband and I can't make it. I'm so sorry to cancel last minute, but my grandmother has had an accident and is in the hospital in San Francisco. We need to stay near home to help with her care."

"I am so sorry," Felicity said, feeling terrible for her guest. The Castles had been renting her cabin every year for the past five years. They were a lovely couple who came to visit with family that lived just outside of Christmas Grove. "I hope your grandmother is going to be okay."

"So do I," Sherry said. "Listen, I've got to go talk to her doctor, but I wanted to let you know so you wouldn't worry when we didn't show up later today."

"Thank you, Sherry. And please send my good wishes to your grandmother. We're going to miss you and your husband this year."

"We'll miss it too," Sherry said. Then she wished Felicity a merry Christmas before ending the call.

Felicity pulled the reservation up on the computer, noting that the Castles had paid in full for their rental. Feeling terrible for them, she immediately processed a refund the orchard couldn't afford and prayed for a Christmas miracle. Even though it was their policy to offer no refunds on canceled rentals within two weeks of the reservation date, the Castles were some of her favorite guests. She couldn't, in good conscience, keep their money when she knew they were dealing with a family emergency.

The miracle she prayed for walked in an hour later.

"Well, hello there, handsome," Marilyn said to Jackson as he strode up to the counter. "What can I do for you today?"

"I need an apple pie and a bottle of that apple cider," he said.

Felicity looked up from her spot where she was restocking the fudge and smiled at the handsome man. "Did you miss me already?"

"Of course," he said, casting his gaze over her from head to toe before he chuckled softly. "I see that you traded the dust for smears of chocolate."

Felicity glanced down at the apron she was wearing and just laughed. He was right. She'd been in the back room cutting up the homemade fudge and had managed to get more of it on the apron than she had into the display case. "It's been a day."

"Tell me about it," he said. "I just found out that I need to find a place to stay for the next two weeks. Since there are no short-term rentals and the inn is full, I'm about to impose on the newlyweds. They were kind enough to offer me their couch until Christmas. That's what the pie and the cider is for. A thank you gift." Then he grimaced. "But my back isn't looking forward to it."

"Wait, what?" Felicity asked. "What's wrong with your house? Did your mother run you off?"

"Sort of," he said. "It's a long story, but the short version is that it's being rented out to film a movie she's in, and I needed to move out for a few weeks."

"And your answer is to stay on Marissa and Danny's couch?" Felicity shook her head. "That sounds miserable."

"Their guest room is full of pottery stock. It's either that or find a place down the mountain, and that commute sounds worse than a couch."

"The cabin's available," Marilyn said helpfully.

"It is?" Jackson asked hopefully. "I didn't see it on the short-term rental sites."

"Our Christmas guests just canceled," Felicity said. "I'll give it to you at half price as a thank you for helping with the lien stuff."

"You don't need to give me a discount," Jackson said, his shoulders sagging in relief. "The fee to rent my house covers outside accommodations. All I need to do is submit an invoice, and they'll handle it."

Felicity nearly cried in relief. She'd spent the past hour crunching numbers and wondering how she was going to pay bills now that she'd refunded two weeks of cabin rental income. "That's fortuitous," she said. "For us, anyway."

"For all of us," he corrected. "Did you really think I wanted to stay with the newlyweds?" He faked a shudder. "Can you imagine what I'd wake up to?"

Felicity laughed. "Okay, that's enough. No one needs to think about that." She reached under the counter and came up with the key to the cabin. "I'll email you an invoice to submit."

Jackson threw down his credit card. "Run this. I'll get them to reimburse me."

"You don't have to do that," Felicity argued. "If they are paying—"

"I can use the mileage points," he said, cutting her off.

It was hard to argue with that. "Okay." She quickly got him squared away and then said, "Just let us know if you need anything. The fridge is already stocked with items our guests had requested. Use what you want and discard the rest."

Jackson nodded. "Thank you, Felicity. You have no idea how much I appreciate this."

"No need to thank anyone. We're just glad to have the cabin rented. Now go settle in and let us get back to work."

He handed Marilyn cash for the pie and cider. "I will, but I'm taking these with me. After the morning I've had, I think pie is definitely in order."

Felicity laughed as she and Marilyn watched him walk out the door.

"It looks like there's plenty of Christmas magic in the air," Marilyn said, her eyebrows raised. "Seems something is trying to make sure you two spend as much time together as possible."

"Magic? Come on, Marilyn," Felicity said, rolling her eyes. "The cabin coming available was just a coincidence. You don't really think that Sherry Castle's grandmother had an accident and was sent to the hospital just so the universe could throw me and Jackson together, do you?"

"No," she said, shaking her head. "That's not how I think things work. But since the cabin was available, I do think something other than coincidence sent Jackson here. This land has always had a way of making sure things turn out right… even when it looks like they won't."

"I pray that's true," Felicity said, thinking of the lien. "You have no idea how much I want to believe that."

Marilyn patted her hand. "You'll see. Something tells me

that Jackson Bell is meant to be part of your story. Whether you want him to be or not."

Felicity kept her gaze focused on the fudge case she was stocking, refusing to meet Marilyn's eyes. If she did, Felicity was certain that her grandmother's oldest friend would see right through her and know that Felicity desperately wished she was right.

CHAPTER 14

"*I*'m headed to the bank," Marilyn said. "I'll be back in about thirty minutes to help you close."

Felicity glanced at her friend and shook her head. "No, go on home afterward. I've got it from here."

"Are you sure?" Marilyn asked as she looked around. They'd had a fairly busy afternoon, and the store needed some attention. In addition to the pastry bar needing to be cleaned, the stock needed to be straightened and the floors mopped. "I don't mind coming back."

"Nah." Felicity waved a hand. Marilyn had been at the shop by herself that morning and had been running all day. Felicity didn't want to wear her out. "Honestly, I'm just gonna close up and take my time getting things in order as I enjoy the quiet."

Marilyn hesitated. "I don't like leaving you with so much work."

"I don't like leaving you alone to run the store like I did

this morning, so we're even," she said with a smile. "Go on and make the deposit before the bank closes and then enjoy your evening. If I don't finish everything tonight, we can deal with it in the morning."

"If you're sure."

"I'm sure." Felicity pointed at the door. "Now go."

Marilyn walked over and gave the younger woman a hug. "Don't stay too late. Especially if it looks like it's going to start snowing."

If it snowed, Felicity imagined she'd knock on the cabin door and join Jackson, but she didn't need to voice that to Marilyn. "I will."

Once Marilyn was gone, Felicity turned to the pastry bar and got to work wiping everything down. She was going to need to restock her Holiday Cheer again sometime soon, but they had enough to get them through the next day or so. What she really needed to do was pull some pies from the freezer.

After checking to be sure no customers were in the store, Felicity hurried to the back room and pulled out a dozen apple pies. After loading them on a cart, she returned to the store, finding a tall, dark-haired man standing just inside the entrance of the store.

He turned when he heard her coming and flashed her a brilliant smile. "Hello."

Felicity stared at the beautiful man, a little mesmerized by his Hollywood good looks. "Are you an actor?" she blurted and then clamped her mouth shut, feeling like a fool.

The man chuckled. "Sorry to disappoint. I'm just a guy who's here visiting family."

"Right." Felicity pushed the cart behind the pastry counter and walked over to him. "How can I help you?"

"Are all the apple products made with produce from the orchard, or do you bring some in from outside sources?" he asked.

"Everything is made with our own apples," Felicity said, her chest swelling with pride. "We also make our own fudge and chocolates, but obviously we import the chocolate for that."

He nodded. "Impressive. Can I get two pies and a pound of your most popular fudge?"

"Sure." Felicity got busy packaging his items and then rang him up at the register. When she told him his total, he raised both eyebrows.

"That's pretty steep," he said.

She shrugged one shoulder. "Not really, considering we use the highest quality ingredients and everything is handmade."

"And you sell enough pie and fudge to keep you in business all year?" he asked, sounding skeptical.

Felicity clamped her mouth shut, willing herself to swallow a snarky reply. Why he thought she was going to tell a perfect stranger her business was beyond her. "We're still here, aren't we?"

"You certainly are," he said as he glanced around the shop. After he used his card to pay for his purchases, he nodded to her. "Have a good night, Ms. Hill."

As the man exited the store, Felicity frowned. How had he known her last name? While anyone who lived or worked in Christmas Grove would know her, it was weird that a perfect stranger had that information. Though he had said he was in town visiting family. They could have mentioned it. But how had he known she wasn't just an employee?

The question nagged at her while she finished restocking the pastry bar.

By the time she straightened the merchandise and mopped the floor, Felicity had completely forgotten about the nosy stranger. But after she locked up and was walking toward her Jeep, she spotted someone walking down the road that led to the cabin. "Jackson? Is that you?"

No answer.

She peered through the darkness, her heart starting to race. Jackson was supposed to be at Sleighed, working. And the person who was now walking toward her was taller and slimmer with a different gait. Whoever it was, it certainly wasn't Jackson Bell.

Felicity positioned her keys so that they were poking out of her knuckles and moved to stand right next to her Jeep. She touched the door handle, unlocking the vehicle, and then waited to see who was skulking around her property.

The person walked across the parking lot, heading for the white SUV that was parked right in front of the store. Felicity stayed quiet, watching, and when the man got to his vehicle, she wasn't all that surprised to realize he was the man she'd assumed was some sort of actor. The one who'd asked if they sold enough product to stay open all year. The one who'd known her last name.

What in the world was he up to?

"Are you lost?" she asked.

He froze and then let out a soft chuckle. "You startled me."

"I startled you?" she replied incredulously. "I'm not the one skulking around in the dark on someone else's property."

"I'm hardly skulking," he said, sounding amused. "I heard there was a cabin rental here, and all I did was go check it out to see if I might want to stay there sometime."

She narrowed her eyes at him, wondering why this man was ruffling all her feathers. "There are pictures online."

"I know," he said. "I saw them. It's a nice place. Maybe I'll book it sometime." Then without another word, he climbed into the white SUV and backed out of the parking space.

Felicity stood by her Jeep, waiting for the SUV to disappear down the long driveway. Just as the vehicle was starting to round the corner, a loud crack reverberated through the silence and a large pine tree fell right on the road, barely missing the SUV. Shocked into complete silence, Felicity stood frozen for just a moment before she took off at a dead run.

The man jumped out of his SUV and ran to take a look at the tree that was lying just behind his car. Then he started to yell. "This tree almost killed me!"

Felicity's heart was nearly beating right out of her chest, and a cold sweat had broken out over her skin. If that tree had fallen only a moment sooner... She couldn't even think about the consequences. "Are you all right?" she huffed out when she was about ten feet from the man.

"I almost died!" he cried.

Felicity stopped and stared at him, giving him a look of exasperation. "The tree didn't hit you or your car."

"If I'd been going five miles an hour slower, it most certainly would have. Do you have any idea how much of a liability it is having diseased trees on your property?" He was fuming, walking back and forth as he ranted.

"Pardon me, but my trees are not diseased." She walked over to the pine and peered at it through the darkness. It was impossible to tell what had happened, but when she poked at the stump, it wasn't soft in any way, and it made zero sense to Felicity why the tree might have fallen. It wasn't windy and as far as she knew, there wasn't a pest problem on the property. At least there hadn't been the last time they'd done an inspection, which would have been in the fall during harvest time.

"Obviously something is wrong if your tree just fell with no other cause," he huffed.

"Well, that's my issue, now isn't it?" Felicity shot back, her nerves frayed. The close call had shaken her to her core. "I assure you that we'll get to the root cause of why this tree fell. Beyond that, there isn't much more I can do right now."

He glared at her and then climbed back into his SUV before peeling off down the road.

Felicity stood in the dark, watching until his taillights faded, and then turned and knelt beside the tree. She took her phone out of her pocket and engaged the flashlight so she could see the split of the tree better. Both the stump and the trunk were jagged, but once again she confirmed that neither were soft. Confused, she stood and started to walk back to her storage shed. That tree would need to be moved if she wanted to leave that night. Or if Jackson was going to get back to the cabin.

Just as she took a few steps, she felt magic brush up against her skin. It was the light, airy magic that she often felt during the harvest, the kind that indicated the woodland fairies were nearby.

"Did you do this?" she called out.

The magic intensified for just a second as she heard the faint tinkling of laughter.

Felicity let out a sigh. "Thank you for watching over me. But scaring guests like that isn't going to help."

The laughter vanished, but the magic remained, and this time it felt like a warm hug.

"I know you're just trying to protect me. Thank you. But now I need to get the chainsaw out and cut up that tree before I can go meet Jackson."

There was silence for a moment before she heard a faint, "Sorry," off in the distance.

The magic vanished and she knew the woodland fairies had disappeared.

Feeling both a little amused and a little annoyed, she went to the shed, got her chainsaw and a battery-operated lantern, and got to work.

CHAPTER 15

*J*ackson made one last swipe on the grill as an ache settled between his shoulders. It was pushing ten o'clock on a Monday, a day that he was usually finished cleaning up five minutes after the kitchen closed at 9 p.m. But that night had been something else. Starting at about 7:30, orders started streaming in and just didn't stop until Marissa declared the kitchen was closed.

By the time Jackson got everything cleaned up and restocked for the following day, he was more than ready for a beer or two. After washing up and changing into a clean long-sleeved T-shirt, he emerged from the kitchen and scanned the bar until his gaze landed on the gorgeous blonde he'd been anxious to see ever since she'd agreed to a drink with him after work.

Jackson walked up behind Felicity, who was sitting with Clara, and said, "Hey, gorgeous."

She turned and gave him a tired smile. "Hey, you. Busy night."

He took the empty stool and gave Marissa a grateful nod when she placed a beer in front of him. As he took a sip, he glanced around and held back a grimace when he spotted his mother Eva sitting with Larry the director. There were also a few tables filled with beautiful people and a few more with what looked to be the production crew for Larry's movie. They were all wearing jeans and sweatshirts without an ounce of glam. Meanwhile, the beautiful people were wearing designer duds and were made up to the nines.

"Definitely busy. Looks like the movie people found Sleighed," he said.

"And thank the goddess for that," Marissa said as she leaned on the bar. "This is the busiest Monday since I don't even know when. If that Larry guy keeps ordering top shelf drinks, we're going to make our monthly quota in one night."

"Sounds like a merry Christmas indeed," Felicity said.

"Is this seat taken?" a man with perfectly white teeth and wearing a button-down shirt with a sweater vest asked Clara.

She glanced up at him, her face flushing with pleasure as she said, "It is now."

The man gave her a half smile and sat, turning to face her. "Which brilliant casting director tapped you for this movie?"

"Me?" Clara clamped a hand over her chest and laughed. "I'm not an actress."

"You're not?" He shifted his gaze over her appreciatively. "How did that happen? You have a face that was just born to be on the big screen."

"Goddess above," Felicity whispered to Jackson. "Can this dude lay it on any thicker?"

Jackson supposed he could, and likely would, if he thought he had a chance of taking Clara home that night. The guy was in full-court-press mode.

"Stop," Clara said, grinning at him. "I'm a glass artist. I assume you're an actor?"

"Glass artist?" The man's demeanor changed from flirty douche to one of pure interest. "Seriously? You blow glass for a living?"

"I do." She held out her hand. "I'm Clara Bowen, and I own Holidaze Glassworks."

"Hudson Snow. Actor." He took her hand in his and then held it for a moment longer than necessary as he added, "It's nice to meet you, Clara Bowen. I'd love to see your work sometime."

"Same," Clara said, clearly getting lost in the man's dark eyes.

Felicity turned to Jackson and gave him a knowing smile. "Looks like Clara's gonna be busy for the rest of the night."

"Good thing I'm here then," he said, giving her a wink.

She laughed and then leaned into him, closing her eyes. "It's been one heck of a day."

"You can say that again," he agreed as he wrapped an arm around her shoulders, enjoying her warmth. If he had his way, he'd finish his beer and then immediately take her back to the cabin he was renting. This time he wouldn't be as chivalrous as he'd been the night they'd been snowed in.

This time he'd show her what they were both missing by keeping their distance.

"Eva! Larry!" a slick man wearing all black called out as he walked in the pub. He made a beeline for Jackson's mother and the producer and clasped Larry on the back before grabbing a chair, turning it around, and straddling it as he sat.

"Ugh," Felicity said. "That guy again."

"You know him?" Jackson asked, giving her his full attention.

"Yes," she said. "Well, no, not exactly. He came by the store right before I closed. He purchased a few things, asked a couple of questions, and then later, I found him wandering around the property."

Jackson's senses were on high alert. "What kind of questions?"

"He just asked if we managed to turn a profit. I didn't answer. It's none of his business."

"Of course it isn't." Jackson turned to eye the stranger and did his best to keep his expression neutral. There was only one reason in his mind that someone would be asking about profits and checking out the property. This man was scoping out the business opportunities of Apples and Spice and Everything Nice. Was he the one behind the lien? Or was he a prospective buyer who was poised to take over the property once it was foreclosed?

"Anyway, the woodland fairies didn't like him either," Felicity said with a soft laugh.

"They don't? How do you know?" he asked.

"They scared him by making a tree fall. It barely missed his car. Now he's all butt hurt about it, but there was no damage, so there's nothing he can do about it."

Jackson stared at her open-mouthed. "Do they do that kind of thing often?"

"No, not at all," she said, shaking her head. "It's very unusual, but considering their reaction, I'm going to say that they don't want him to come back... ever."

"Do they visit often?" he asked, wondering if his visit in the woods with the Christmas fairy was a regular thing.

"The fairies? Oh no. Only when they think they need to protect the property... or the family, I suppose. I've never even seen them, only heard and felt them. But my grandmother used to see them in the early days, right after they started the orchard. The fairies loved my grandparents. Said they approved of them being guardians of the land."

A swell of pride filled Jackson's chest. The fact that the Christmas fairy had come to him to ask him for help made him feel a weight of responsibility that he wouldn't take lightly. What was it she'd said? That he needed to help Felicity find her Christmas spirit. He thought he'd done a fairly good job of that the night they'd taken the sleigh ride, but he wouldn't stop there. He'd do everything in his power to make sure that Felicity had the best Christmas season ever.

"Felicity Hill," a man said from behind them.

Jackson turned and spotted the man who'd been skulking around her property. His fists flexed, and he had an urge to grab the man by his silk shirt, haul him outside, and demand to know who sent him.

Felicity looked up at him. "It puts me at a disadvantage that you know my name, but I don't know yours."

"No? I thought I already introduced myself," he said with a slight air of superiority, and Jackson knew the man was messing with her, trying to get and keep the upper hand. But for what? Just to put her off guard?

Jackson had no use for the man, but he couldn't just ignore him. Not if he had something to do with the lien.

"Trace Rhodes," the man said. Then he turned to look at Larry and Eva. "Hey, Larry. Come over here. There's someone I want you to meet."

Larry rose with Eva hot on his heels. She looked like a puppy following her owner around, and it made Jackson's stomach turn. He hated the way his mother was fawning all over Larry. It made him wonder what else she'd done to get her part besides offer up his house as a filming location.

"Hey, buddy," Trace said to Larry. "I want you to meet Felicity Hill. She's the owner of Apples and Spice and Everything Nice, the place I was telling you about."

Jackson tensed.

Felicity raised her eyebrows and looked back and forth between the two men. "Oh yeah? And what exactly did you say about my orchard, Trace Rhodes?"

"He said it's the perfect place for filming," Larry said. "Trace is the production manager on the film we're making.

It sounds like he found the cabin and magical forest we're looking for."

"You want to film at the cabin?" Jackson blurted. "The one I'm staying at after I've been run out of my house?"

Larry blinked at Jackson and then let out a loud laugh. "That's quite the coincidence, isn't it? But don't worry, Jackson. We don't need to film inside. Just outside." He turned to Felicity. "If the property is as good as Trace says, I'd love to do business with you."

Felicity glanced at Jackson, and he could almost read her thoughts. If the money was good enough to displace Jackson for a few weeks, it was likely worth her while to hear them out. "Fine. Come by tomorrow and we'll talk."

"Excellent," Larry said, lighting up like a Christmas tree. "I'll be there first thing." He squeezed her arm and then wrapped an arm around Trace's shoulders as the two walked out.

Eva hesitated, placing her hand on Jackson's shoulder. "Thank you, Jackson."

He just nodded, not knowing what else to say to her. She'd gotten what she wanted. What more could she want from him?

His mother looked like she wanted to say something else, but instead, she clamped her mouth shut, lowered her head, and then walked out of the pub.

"Is she all right?" Felicity asked him.

He shrugged. "I assume so."

"The director is using her," Felicity said.

He met her gaze. "I'm pretty sure they're using each other."

She frowned. "That's… sad."

He nodded his agreement.

"Come on." Felicity stood. "Let's go."

He stared up into her pretty face. "Where?"

"Home." She slipped her hand into his and tugged.

Jackson let her tug him out of the pub and didn't question her when she led him to her Jeep.

CHAPTER 16

Felicity was tired of fighting it. All she wanted to do was fall into Jackson's arms and forget about everything else. Forget about the lien. The producer who wanted to film on her land. The fact that her business was barely treading water due to a bad crop a few years ago.

And she certainly didn't want to be at home when Clara brought that pretty boy home from the bar. Instead, she headed back to the orchard.

"The cabin is home?" Jackson asked, giving her a sexy half smile.

"It's *your* home for now," she quipped.

"You do realize we left my truck back at Sleighed, right?"

She glanced over at him, giving him an incredulous look. "Are you really worried about your truck right now?"

"No." His lips twitched as if he was trying not to laugh.

"Good. I'll take you to work tomorrow. Or to your truck

in the morning if you have places to be. But right now, I don't give a damn. Do you?"

"Nope," he said, grinning at her openly now.

Felicity smiled at him and then focused on the road. Once she pulled into the drive that led to the cabin, her entire body started to relax. There was just something about being on her property that settled her. It always had.

And the fact that Jackson didn't upset that feeling was something she couldn't ignore. Every other man she'd dated, she'd always had the urge to send them packing when they were at the orchard.

Jackson was different.

Not that they were dating. But even she could admit that there was *something* going on between them.

Something she no longer wanted to ignore.

She parked in front of the cabin and turned the Jeep off.

Without a word, Jackson exited the vehicle and came around to Felicity's side, opening her door. He held his hand out to her and asked, "Shall we?"

Felicity let him tug her out of the Jeep and then she stood right in front of him, staring up at him. "What is it about you that always seems to shatter my defenses?"

"Is that what I do?"

She nodded. "I don't know what to make of it."

"Me neither," he said softly as he brushed a lock of her hair behind one ear. "But I can't say I'm unhappy about it."

Felicity smiled softly. "Me neither." Then she turned and led him up the steps to the cabin. "You don't mind if I stay over, do you?"

"Tonight? I wouldn't have it any other way."

"Good." She waited while he unlocked the door.

The cabin was chilly, but Jackson didn't stop to light a fire in the fireplace. Instead, he led her straight to the bedroom.

She slipped her cold hands under his jacket and wrapped her arms around his waist. "You're warm."

"I need a shower," he said. "After working in the kitchen all night, I'm pretty sure I smell like a hamburger and fries."

She chuckled softly. "Maybe just a little bit. How about I join you in that shower?"

Jackson let out a small growl and quickly pulled her into the bathroom.

Felicity got the water started, and then when she turned to Jackson, her breath caught. He was still fully clothed, but the heat in his eyes was enough to light a fire in her belly. "If you keep looking at me like that, we're not going to make it into the shower."

"Oh, we're definitely going to make it into the shower." There was a devilish glint in his eyes as he added, "It's just a matter of when."

She fanned herself, pretending to overheat, even though the bathroom was still chilly enough to give her gooseflesh.

"Come here," he said, pulling her closer. As the steam filled the bathroom, Jackson gently turned her around and then took his time removing her sweater as he nuzzled her neck, pressing soft kisses over her skin.

Felicity leaned back into him, soaking up his warmth, reveling in it, memorizing every touch. He was worshipping her, making her feel treasured. It was a feeling she wasn't used to. A feeling she craved.

"Jackson?" she whispered.

"Yes?" His hands froze on her hips.

"You feel better than you should."

He chuckled softly against her skin and continued to undress her. Once she was completely bare, she returned the favor.

Any other man would have taken that as his cue to ravish her in the shower, but when Jackson guided her under the warm spray, he took his time running his hands over her skin and then carefully washing every inch of her. And as the soap suds were being washed away, she took the soap from him and lathered him up, memorizing the feel of his well-defined muscles as well as every dip and scar he carried on his gorgeous body.

"You should come with a warning label," she said softly.

He smirked. "A warning for what?"

"For being so hot. I mean, it should be illegal to look that good naked. You're giving me a complex."

"Oh, come on," he said, shaking his head. "You know you're gorgeous."

She just shrugged. Felicity didn't have any complaints, but it wasn't like she looked as if she worked out on a regular basis. Not like Jackson did. The man could have been on the cover of a fireman's calendar.

Felicity licked her lips thinking about it.

Jackson turned the water off and handed her a towel.

They both quickly dried off and then without a word, Jackson picked her up and carried her to the bed.

After they climbed in, Jackson propped his head up with his hand and stared down at her, his gaze reverent. "You're the most beautiful woman I've ever known."

"You're flattering me," she whispered.

"I'm just being honest." Then he lowered his head and claimed her lips in a searing kiss.

Felicity instantly got lost in him. This was more than just desire. His touch went deeper than just her flesh, finding a way to somehow penetrate her soul.

He pulled away for just a brief moment, his hand tangling in her hair. "Are you sure about this?"

Felicity nodded. "I wouldn't have invited myself over if I hadn't wanted you tonight."

"No, Felicity," he said, searching her gaze. "I mean are you sure about us. I can't just be your one-night stand again. I'm in too deep now. Please tell me you're not going to push me away when you wake up in the morning."

A lump got caught in Felicity's throat as she tried and failed to speak. Finally, she forced out, "I can't make any promises about the future, Jackson, but I can say that I'm done pushing you away."

Relief flashed in Jackson's dark eyes just before he claimed her lips again.

Felicity wrapped herself around him, finally ready to fully give herself body and soul to the only man she'd ever trusted.

LIGHT STREAMED in the small window, splashing a ray of light over Jackson's handsome features. Felicity lay next to him, her head sharing the same pillow as she gazed at him, taking in his peaceful, relaxed slumber.

In the quiet of the morning, she'd never felt more content. And she knew that deep down that should scare her, but it didn't. She just prayed that her gut was right when it told her Jackson wasn't like other men. That he wouldn't leave… like her father. Because no matter how much she might want to deny it, she couldn't hide from the truth.

Felicity Hill was falling for Jackson Bell.

"Morning," Jackson said without even opening his eyes.

"How did you know I was awake?" she asked, trailing her fingers over his bare chest.

His eyes fluttered open. "The sound of your breathing. It's deeper and more rhythmic when you're asleep."

"Can't get anything by you," she said and then kissed him.

"Hmm," he murmured and then grabbed her around the waist, twisting them so that she was beneath him.

Grinning up at him, she said, "Now what?"

"Remember what we did last night?" He pumped his eyebrows suggestively.

"Did something happen last night?" she asked innocently.

"Yes. And it's about to happen again," he said with a growl before he bent his head and nipped at her neck.

"A girl could get used to this," she said with a happy sigh, but then she groaned a moment later when her phone started to ring.

"Don't answer it," Jackson said, his hands moving down her sides as he dropped open-mouth kisses on the swell of her breast.

"I have to." She grabbed her phone that was sitting on the nightstand. "It could be Marilyn or—" Felicity let out a gasp. "Stop. It's Doris."

"The lady at the assessor's office?" Jackson asked.

"Yes." She rolled out from underneath Jackson and answered the call. "Doris? Do you have something for me?"

"Yes, dear. I found the paperwork you're looking for. I have copies waiting for you."

"Perfect!" Felicity said. "We'll be right down." She ended the call and hopped out of bed, letting out a hiss when the cold air hit her bare skin. Still, she glanced at Jackson. "Come on. Put your pants on. Doris has the goods."

He followed her out of the bed. Ten minutes later, they were dressed, in the Jeep, and headed toward the courthouse.

"Coffee?" Jackson asked as they got close to the drive-thru coffee trailer that was painted like the Polar Express.

"Already headed that way," she said, flashing him a tired smile. "Someone kept me up way past my bedtime. I'm pretty sure the only way I'm making it through this day is with copious amounts of caffeine."

"Regrets?" he asked.

Felicity looked over at him, her heart full as she said, "Not one."

His face lit up with a sweet smile as he reached over and placed his hand on her leg. "Me neither."

CHAPTER 17

Felicity felt... *right*. She couldn't explain it. As she and Jackson made their way into town, she just had a feeling that she was exactly where she was supposed to be, with the person she was supposed to be with, doing the thing she was supposed to be doing.

Did that mean they were going to resolve the issue with the lien that day? Goddess above, she hoped so. A tingle of anticipation bloomed in her gut, and she pressed into the gas, making the Jeep go that much faster.

She swung into the lot where the train-shaped coffee trailer was and headed for the drive-thru. Jackson was right. The day called for copious amounts of caffeine. Of course, that meant that the line was ten cars deep when she pulled in behind a truck, and she let out an irritated sigh. "I should have just let you make coffee at the cabin."

"It probably would have been faster, but then we

wouldn't have been able to get donuts, so I suppose it's a trade-off." He reached over and took her hand in his.

Felicity stared down at their entwined fingers as he stroked his thumb over the back of her hand and decided it was worth stopping for both the donuts and the quiet moment they were sharing.

She shook her head at herself. Since when had she become a complete sap? Probably sometime between their intimate shower that had been all about caring for each other and when Jackson had carried her to bed. Never in her life had she felt safer with someone. More loved. More cherished.

"I know what you're thinking," Jackson said.

She raised both eyebrows at him. "You think so? Go ahead, tell me."

"You're thinking you better get two maple bars. One for now and one for after we talk to Doris."

Felicity tilted her head back and laughed. "Is that your way of saying that *you* want more than one donut?"

"Maybe," he said, his eyes twinkling with mischief. "Did it work?"

"Yes." The line inched forward and Felicity let up on the brake, letting the Jeep roll forward.

"Oh, good. Maybe we should get a half dozen and bring a couple to Doris," he said.

"I'm sensing that you might be a little bit of a donut addict," she mused.

"An addict who likes to share." He grinned at her.

"You're too much," she said, but when they got to the

window, not only did she order extra donuts, she also got a peppermint latte for Doris as a thank you for helping them out.

Five minutes later, they walked into the assessor's office with two donuts and the latte.

Doris looked up from her spot at her desk and said wistfully, "Good morning. Looks like someone's a lucky elf today. That coffee and whatever's in that bag is making my mouth water."

"We're glad you think so," Felicity said, putting the white bag of donuts on her desk and handing her the latte. "Because these are for you."

"Me?" She pressed her hand to her chest. "Are you serious?" Her eyes misted with joyful tears as she peeked into the bag. "This was so kind of you."

"I just wanted to show my appreciation for you looking for that paperwork for me. You have no idea how important it is."

"I was just doing my job," Doris said as she let out an embarrassed chuckle. "Look at me, crying over donuts. You'd think no one had ever done anything nice for me before. It's just that ever since my Bobby passed a few years ago, I haven't exactly had anyone to dote on me, and it's nice to be thought of every once in a while."

Felicity and Jackson shared a quick glance, and Felicity wondered when the last time was that anyone had taken a second to think about or appreciate Doris. She reached over and squeezed the older woman's hand. "I'm sorry about your husband."

"You're so sweet. Thank you." Doris wiped at her eyes and laughed. "I'm sorry. Let me get you that paperwork. I made copies for you."

"Thank you," Felicity said.

Jackson pressed his hand to the small of her back and whispered, "See. Everyone likes donuts."

She nodded but knew that the gesture was what had been important to Doris, and the fact that this man had thought to brighten someone else's day made Felicity wonder why she'd been pushing him away for so long.

You know why, the voice in her head said.

But she ignored it, determined not to self-sabotage the moment.

"Here you go," Doris said, placing a manila folder on the counter. "I hope this helps."

Jackson took the envelope, pulled one of the papers halfway out, and then grinned at Doris. "My dear, you're a miracle worker. This is exactly what we needed. Thank you."

Felicity stared at him, anticipation nearly eating her alive. "It really has the information we need?"

"It does." He tugged her toward the door. Just as they reached the exit, Jackson glanced over his shoulder. "Thank you, Doris. Have a wonderful holiday, okay?"

Doris held up the donut she'd just taken a bite of and mumbled something that sounded a lot like, "I will now."

"Someone should invite Doris to the Christmas ball," Felicity said as they climbed back into her Jeep.

"If you mean me," Jackson joked, "I've already got a date."

Felicity rolled her eyes but still chuckled. "No, I didn't mean you. I have plans for you, sir. But it would be nice to see her all dressed up and having fun, don't you think? We should work on it."

"You really want to set up Doris?" he asked. "How do you know she doesn't already have a date?"

Felicity gave him a slightly exasperated look. "You heard her. She said she hasn't had anyone paying her attention since her husband passed. If she had a beau, she wouldn't have said that. And honestly, if she does, she needs to trade him in on a new model, because he's not worth the hassle if he's not doting on her."

"Can't argue there." Jackson took the paperwork out of the manila envelope and said, "I have the name of the original lienholder. Hold on. Let me search the internet for his current address." Jackson pulled out his phone, tapped the screen a few times, and then said, "Got it. Head north. He's a few miles out of town up in the hills."

Felicity put the Jeep in gear and eased out onto the road as Jackson programmed her GPS. "What's his name?" she asked.

"Ernie Sinclair. Does that ring any bells?"

"Ernie Sinclair," Felicity repeated. "You know, I think my grandmother had a friend named Ernie. I never met him, but she used to talk about him coming over to help her split wood after my grandfather died."

"Sounds promising," Jackson said and then gave his full attention to his phone as he researched the man in question.

Just as they pulled up to a set of wrought iron gates, Jackson said, "This Ernie guy has had quite the career."

"Really? What is he, a loan shark?" Felicity asked, tapping into that dark place inside of herself that always went for the worst-case scenario first.

Jackson smirked. "You think that loaning your grandmother money for the orchard was just the start of a long and sordid career that resulted in busted kneecaps? Here in Christmas Grove?"

"You never know," she said with a sniff. "There are shady people everywhere, Jackson."

"True," he agreed. "But if he was that bad, I doubt this would be the first time you'd heard of him."

Felicity shrugged. He was probably right, but she'd always found it better to be prepared for just about anything. She lowered her window and pressed a button on the security panel. Almost immediately, the buzzer sounded and the gate started to open without anyone asking them who they were or why they were there. She glanced over at Jackson. "Doesn't look like he takes security too seriously."

Jackson looked up and said, "There are at least three cameras recording who comes and goes from this place. I'd say he takes it seriously enough."

Felicity wasn't sure what to make of the security, but all she cared about was the fact that they'd gotten past the gates. If they'd finally found the person they were looking for and couldn't get in, she'd have gone out of her mind.

They parked in front of a gorgeous mountain retreat that was made of wood and stone with plenty of picture windows. They walked up onto the massive front porch, and Felicity smiled at the wooden swing that held both a folded blanket and a pillow, indicating that it wasn't just for decoration. Someone regularly sat out there enjoying the beauty that the mountain retreat had to offer.

Jackson pressed the doorbell, and not a moment later, the door opened to an older gentleman in a sweater and slacks smiling at them.

"Well, hello there," he said, his watery eyes welcoming.

"Hello, sir. You wouldn't happen to be Ernie Sinclair, would you?" Jackson asked.

The man chuckled softly. "Yes, but I don't know why that's a surprise when you're standing on my doorstep." He turned to Felicity and gave her a kind smile. "It's not often I get visitors. Especially when one of those visitors is Kitty's granddaughter."

Felicity blinked at him. "You know who I am?"

"Of course. Come on in. I'll get the Christmas cookies out." He held the door open for them, waiving them into the large foyer. "This way."

Jackson took Felicity's hand, and the warmth of his touch calmed her. She couldn't recall ever meeting Ernie Sinclair, and it was disconcerting that he knew her while she knew nothing about him other than the few facts that Jackson had found online.

Ernie led them into a cozy living room where a fire was crackling in the fireplace. "Have a seat. I'll find some refreshments."

Felicity didn't think there was any way she could put

anything in her stomach. Not with the way her nerves were jumping around, but she supposed it would be nice to have something to keep her hands busy.

While they waited, Felicity focused on the man's large Christmas tree that sat dead center in front of one of the large windows. The lights were twinkling softly around the elegant red and gold ornaments. Someone had gone through a lot of trouble to pick out ornaments to turn his tree into something spectacular, but it was missing that touch of home, the things that make a tree special to each family. There weren't any handmade ornaments or garland. No pictures. No old class projects. Not even anything that indicated it was a treasured piece that had been handed down through the generations.

No, this tree looked like something out of a high-end department store. And while it was beautiful, it was missing history, and roots, and that thing that made Christmas *special*. Not that she blamed him. She hadn't been excited about Christmas for years herself, but then if she'd had her way, she wouldn't have put up a tree at all.

Ernie returned with a wooden tray filled with fancy holiday cookies that looked like they'd come from a bakery and three mugs of hot cocoa. "Help yourself."

Felicity eyed the snowflake-shaped cookies with their powder blue icing and delicate snowflake pattern and decided she couldn't do it. At least not until they asked Ernie about the lien. Instead, she picked up one of the mugs and held it in her hands as she turned to the older man.

He smiled kindly at her. "You are the spitting image of Kitty when she was your age. Do you know that?"

"Um, Marilyn tells me that often enough. I figured she was just trying to flatter me."

Ernie chuckled. "Marilyn, that's a name I haven't heard in years. She and Kitty always were tight. Us older folks sometimes have senior moments, but I can assure you, she's correct. It's like looking back in time. Except Kitty wore her hair differently, and she always wore dresses, even in the winter."

He was right. Kitty Hill had great legs, and she'd known it. She wore skirts and dresses practically every day of her life except when she was working out in the orchard. Even in the winter, she just wore tights to keep her knees from getting frostbite.

"How did you know my grandmother?" Felicity asked, curious now. The man obviously had fond memories of her.

"How did I know Kitty?" he repeated as he stared into the fire. "Well, I guess you could say she's the one who got away." He turned to meet Felicity's eyes. "You see, I was your grandfather's best friend back in the day. Benjamin and I grew up next door to each other outside of Sacramento, and when we met Kitty, we were both smitten. Needless to say, she chose him. It was the second worst day of my life."

There was a ruefulness to his tone, and she wondered what the actual worst day of his life was, but she didn't ask. She'd just met the man and didn't want to pry. "But you stayed friends with them?"

"Of course," he said, sounding surprised. "Benji and I…

Well, we were like brothers. And when he got sick, he made me promise to take care of Kitty for him. I agreed. Back then, I thought that meant that I'd marry her." His chuckle was soft as he shook his head. "But she wasn't interested in that. No, all she wanted was to run the orchard they'd purchased together and make Benji's dream come true. And she did."

"With a little help from you?" Felicity asked.

"Well, sure," he said with a nod. "When she'd let me. Your grandmother was a proud woman."

"Yes, she was. That's why I don't understand this." Felicity pulled the lien paperwork out of her purse and thrust it at him. "There is no way Kitty Hill would have taken a loan and then not paid it back."

"You're right about that," he said even before he looked at the copy of the lien she'd handed him. After he slid his glasses on and actually did scan it, his brow wrinkled as he studied the paperwork. "What is this?"

"You don't know?" Jackson asked. "Is that not one of the companies you own that's listed there as the lienholder?"

Ernie blinked rapidly as if trying to clear his vision and then narrowed his eyes as he read it again. When he looked up, he pulled his glasses off and nodded. "That is my company, but I don't handle the day-to-day business anymore. My nephew does that."

"Listen, Ernie," Felicity said, leaning forward. "I'm one hundred percent certain that this has to be a mistake. Kitty Hill always paid her debts. Can you do something to help us get this lien removed?"

Ernie handed the paperwork back to Felicity. "It's true that I did loan your grandmother money. But did she pay it back? I'd have to believe that she did, but even back then, I wasn't handling the accounting. I was too busy expanding my winery business and then later, my real estate development company. Day-to-day finances weren't on my radar. And honestly, Kitty and I drifted apart until years later when we started meeting up for lunch once a month."

"You never talked about the loan then?" Felicity asked, trying desperately to get the man to agree to help her.

"No." He shook his head. "We were just two old friends reminiscing about our younger days when Benji was still around." His expression turned sad when he added, "Then Kitty passed, and that really was the worst day of my life. You see, I always imagined growing old with her. That someday she'd decide that marrying me wasn't a betrayal to Benji, and then we'd be spending our golden years together. But the universe had other plans. I often wonder what my life might have been like if I hadn't fallen for Kitty. Maybe I'd have my own epic love story and be living out my golden days with a beautiful granddaughter to visit."

"Ernie," Felicity pleaded, "I had no idea about this loan until this foreclosure paperwork showed up the other night. I assure you, that if there is an outstanding loan, I will do everything in my power to pay you back. But the interest that's listed, that's out of reach. If your nephew goes through with this, I'm going to lose my family's orchard. Is that what you want? For me to lose everything?"

The older man studied her and then smiled gently. "I'm

sure you're right about Kitty paying this loan back. She hated owing anyone anything. Especially me," he said with a chuckle. "I have no doubt this is just a mistake." He got up, went to a desk that was against a far wall, and pulled out a business card. When he returned, he handed it to Felicity. "Call Vincent and make an appointment. I'm sure he can help you get this all straightened out."

Felicity stared at the card. It just had the name Vincent Sinclair and a phone number listed. "Will I have trouble getting an appointment?"

He shook his head. "I'll call his assistant and tell her to expect your call."

Ernie walked them to the door. Once they were on the porch, they said their goodbyes.

"Thank you," Felicity said. "For the help and for caring enough about my grandmother to help her. Even if you hadn't told us, I would have known you cared deeply for her."

"Kitty was one of a kind." Then Ernie squeezed her arm and said, "I have a feeling you take after her. Good luck, Felicity Hill. And call me if you ever need anything. Kitty and Benji would be proud of you."

Felicity thanked him again, and then on impulse gave the older man a hug. He held on tighter than she'd expected, and by the time they broke apart, they both had watery eyes. She smiled gratefully at him and then let Jackson lead her back to the Jeep.

"That seemed productive," Jackson said as he held her door open for her.

"It did," she agreed as she climbed in. "Let's hope this Vincent guy is as helpful as Ernie thinks he is. Because I'm ready to think about other things... like what you're going to be wearing to the Christmas ball."

"You're interested in what I'm going to wear?" he asked with a laugh.

"I'm more interested in what I'm going to be peeling off you at the end of the night," she said, flashing him a flirty smile. "But I won't lie. You dressed up in a suit is definitely something I'm looking forward to seeing."

"I see. Well, I'll just have to up my game then, won't I?"

Felicity licked her lips and nodded.

Jackson leaned in, gave her a lingering kiss, and then pulled back. "Do that again and we'll be rolling around in the woods."

"It's too cold for that," she said. "Get in. Let's get out of here so we can call this Vincent guy. Then we can talk about rolling around in the woods naked."

Jackson jogged around the Jeep, laughing to himself. When he was buckled in, he said, "You're something else, you know that, Felicity Hill?"

She just winked at him and put the Jeep in gear.

CHAPTER 18

*J*ackson sat at his computer, staring at the research he'd done on Ernie Sinclair. It was true that the man had grown up outside of Sacramento and had moved to Christmas Grove when he was in his twenties. He'd gotten into the winery business, but his real estate development business had been what really put him on the map as a successful businessman.

Ernie had a hand in building up some of the neighborhoods in Christmas Grove, but it was really the development of downtown that had been his specialty. And that hadn't come without controversy. There were more than a couple of articles from the town newspaper archives that portrayed Ernie as ruthless. One story in particular told the tale of Ernie stealing land out from underneath a family that was struggling to pay back taxes and turning that land into a premier winery.

Another article detailed the hostile takeover of a ranch

that ended with an interview with a young girl crying because her favorite horse was sold to the highest bidder.

The man that was depicted in the articles didn't sound anything like the man they'd met that morning, but Jackson knew that successful business people could be deceiving. Some of the most ruthless were the ones who were the most welcoming and kind, getting people to trust them before they snatched everything right out from beneath them.

He prayed that he was wrong and that Ernie Sinclair wasn't that kind of man.

But to be as successful as he was, there had to be some truth to the stories. No businessman with his achievements got that far without getting a little dirty.

Jackson hoped that Ernie had kept his word and called Vincent. He fingered the card that Felicity had given him when he'd offered to call and make the appointment. Since she was busy in the store, he had time before he had to go into work.

There was only one way to find out. He picked up the phone and dialed the number on the card.

"Vincent Sinclair's office," the nasally voice said on the other end of the line. "How may I help you?"

"Hello," Jackson said. "My name is Jackson Bell, and I'm calling on behalf of Felicity Hill. We're hoping to get an appointment to see Mr. Sinclair as soon as possible about some foreclosure paperwork."

"I'm afraid that Mr. Sinclair is unavailable. I can direct you to our lawyers if you need information about a foreclosure."

"No, I don't need the lawyer," Jackson said patiently. "We spoke with Ernie Sinclair this morning. He specifically said for us to talk to Vincent. He should have called to let the office know we'd be in touch."

"I'm not at liberty to discuss the internal workings of the office, Mr. Bell. All I can do is take a message. Would you like to leave your number?"

Jackson swallowed his annoyance and left his number. He could tell by the assistant's tone that he was unlikely to get a call back. He'd spent enough years working with corporate offices to know that someone in Vincent's position didn't talk to anyone who was in foreclosure, and their only hope of getting an audience was if Ernie made good on his promise to call Vincent. After his research, he wasn't at all sure that Ernie would keep his word.

"I'll just have to keep calling," Jackson said to himself. "Or go by the office." The idea was appealing, but he'd give it a little bit of time before he started making a complete nuisance of himself.

The sound of a car door closing caught his attention, and he got up from the kitchen table in the cabin to see who had arrived. As he peered out the front window, he spotted Larry the producer and his sidekick, Trace, getting out of a silver Escalade.

Trace had a phone pressed to his ear while Larry was standing in front of the cabin, gazing at it with a wide smile on his face. The man actually clapped his hands together with glee like a child in a candy store.

Jackson stepped out of the cabin and stood on the front porch. "It looks like you like what you see."

Larry's expression instantly went blank. "I didn't see you there, Jackson."

"That's because I was inside," he said dryly. Larry wasn't fooling him. He loved the orchard and could see his film being shot there. That meant that Felicity could negotiate a decent rate. "When do you need to start filming?"

The director ignored his question and moved into the field past the cabin where rows and rows of apple trees were lined up.

Trace glanced over at Larry and visibly shuddered as the man walked through the trees. "Be careful, Larry. Don't let one of them fall on you!"

Larry waved a hand at Trace and just kept walking.

Jackson took a seat on the front porch, unwilling to let the producers out of his sight. He just wanted to see what they were looking at and what their reactions were. When Larry returned from the orchard, he walked up to Trace and said, "Make the deal with Ms. Hill. You were right. The orchard is perfect."

Trace nodded and followed Larry to the Escalade. The two got in and headed back to the store. Jackson hopped into his truck and followed them. He pulled in right beside the Escalade and watched as Larry wandered off, inspecting the property. He held his hands up in a box shape as if he were studying what a camera shot would look like once he started filming. Jackson caught Trace rolling his eyes just before he skirted around a tree and headed for the store.

Laughing to himself, Jackson followed Trace and walked right up to Felicity as Trace was handing her the contract.

Felicity immediately handed it to him and said, "Can you check the terms and make sure I'm not getting shafted?"

Trace quickly snatched the paperwork back and said, "Wait. Let me make sure it's all correct first."

Jackson swallowed his laugh as Felicity snickered softly.

"I'll be right back." Trace hurried out of the store, nearly tripping over his own feet as he went.

"That was interesting," Felicity said, turning to Jackson. "Was it something I said?" she added jokingly.

"I can't imagine," he deadpanned. He assumed that Trace had tried to lowball Felicity, but once she handed him the contract, Trace had realized that Jackson already had a generous contract and would know the offer wasn't a good one. Jackson just hoped they offered her something fair. He didn't want to spend all day dealing with Trace Rhodes.

When the bell on the door rang again, Trace walked in, a bright smile on his face. He once again handed the paperwork to Felicity, but she didn't even look at it before passing it to Jackson.

"I think you'll find the terms more than fair," Trace told Felicity.

"Jackson Bell is representing me," she said. "Talk to him." Then she stepped away to go ring up a customer who had an entire basket full of gifts to purchase.

After reading every last word of the contract, Jackson took out a pen, crossed out the amount they were offering her, and added fifteen percent. He also jotted down an extra clause that said if they caused any damage to the structures or the orchard, the production company would be liable to pay for repairs or replacements.

Trace gave him a flat stare as he took the paperwork back. After reading the corrections, he clamped his mouth shut. Jackson didn't miss the tension in his jaw as he gave Jackson a slight nod, indicating that he agreed to the terms. Trace stuffed the paperwork into his binder and said, "I'll be right back."

Jackson watched as the man stomped out of the store.

"He doesn't look happy," Felicity said.

"He's not. I got him right up to the upper end of their budget and made them liable for any and all damage. Larry isn't going to be happy with his negotiating skills, but Trace wouldn't have agreed if he hadn't already been authorized to go that high." Jackson stuffed his hands into his jeans pockets and rocked back on his heels, feeling satisfied. "I've done enough deals to know that you got the better end of the bargain."

She eyed him. "How much did you get me?"

After he told her the number, she let out a low whistle. "And that's for just a few days of filming?"

"They say they only need a few days, but you have to be open to them coming back for reshoots," he said.

"I'm open," she said, her arms wide as she grinned up at him. "For that kind of cash? They can film here every year."

He shook his head, amused. "You might want to see how invasive they are before you start signing more contracts, but I agree it seems like easy money." Jackson just kept his fingers crossed that production was well equipped to handle filming on location without any major issues.

The next time the bell rang, Larry and Trace walked in together. Larry walked over to Felicity and held his hand out to her. "You drive a hard bargain, Ms. Hill. But I have to admit that your orchard is gorgeous. It's going to be worth every penny."

"Thank you," she said. "I can't wait to see the movie you're making. When does it come out? Next Christmas?"

"Yes. We're aiming for the weekend after Thanksgiving. I'll expect a gift basket after all the fans come out to see the orchard."

Felicity started to laugh but covered it with a cough as she nodded. "Definitely. When the masses show up, I'll remember who made that possible."

"I look forward to it." Larry gestured for Trace to hand her the paperwork.

She scanned it and then handed it to Jackson for one last look. When he approved it, she signed. Larry signed right after her and then said they'd get her a copy in the mail.

"Oh, no need. I have a copier here. Let me just scan it." She disappeared into the back and returned a minute later with the contract in an envelope. "Thank you, sir. It's been a pleasure."

"It certainly has," Larry said and then mimed tipping a hat. He handed the paperwork to Trace and then strode out.

Trace tucked the envelope into his jacket pocket and started to follow his boss. But after two steps, he ran into… or was he attacked by… a display of greeting cards. Jackson wasn't quite sure. What he did know was that he felt a familiar magic tingling in the air, followed by an intense feeling of disgust.

Trace scrambled to get to his feet while Felicity went over to offer him a hand. "No," he snapped as he pushed the display off him. "I don't know what it is about this place, but it's a true safety hazard. I'm going to have to up the insurance policy to make sure we're covered when the entire crew is here!"

Jackson heard a faint scoff in the background and a whisper that said, "Don't trust him."

"What was that?" Trace asked, glancing around and waving his hands above his head as if he were trying to bat away a fly. "Did someone say something?"

"No," both Felicity and Jackson said at the same time.

He stared at them for a beat and then huffed as he walked out of the store.

Felicity and Jackson both started to laugh, but they were silenced when the magic around them intensified.

"The fairies are here, and they aren't happy," Felicity said.

In Jackson's mind, he heard one of them say, *We don't trust that man. If he comes back, we'll only run him off again.*

"They don't like Trace," Jackson said, stating the obvious.

"I know. But I just don't know if they hate the idea of the movie filming here, too," she said as she glanced around as if looking for the fairies to appear.

The magic in the air suddenly felt lighter, and Jackson said, "I think you have your answer."

She let out a sigh of relief. "Good. We need that money."

The door opened, and Holly Holiday, the town librarian, walked in, full of Christmas cheer. "Hello, Felicity! Merry Christmas."

"Merry Christmas to you, too, Holly. What can I help you with?"

As Felicity helped Holly, Jackson walked out onto the front porch and watched as Larry and Trace climbed into the Escalade and left the property. He felt rather than saw a form materialize beside him. He knew without even needing confirmation that it was Grace, the Christmas fairy.

"You're doing a good job helping Felicity find her Christmas joy," the fairy said.

"I'm trying. She's agreed to go to the Christmas ball with me this weekend," he said.

"Good." The fairy pressed her hand to his arm, making his entire body come alive with her magic. "Bring her on a snowmobile ride tonight under the moonlight. We have something planned for her."

Jackson turned to look at the fairy, but she was already gone, leaving only a trace of her magic behind.

CHAPTER 19

"Where are you taking me?" Felicity asked as Jackson led her away from the cabin and toward the storage shed on the other side of the drive. "I thought we were headed inside where it's warm. Where we can get naked and fall into bed."

It was just after ten at night, and the full moon was shining down on the fresh snow. After she'd closed up the store, she'd gone home to change and found Clara and her pretty boy smooching on the couch. Not wanting to be a third wheel, she cleaned up and headed to Sleighed again.

It wasn't exactly a hardship. She'd planned to find her way back to the cabin before the night was over anyway, but she hadn't expected to look like an impatient teenager waiting for her boyfriend to get off work. But that's what she'd felt like, and she realized after she'd finished a glass of wine that she didn't even care.

Marissa had teased her good naturedly, but when she

didn't get a rise out of Felicity, she'd let it go and said she was proud of her friend for giving Jackson a chance.

Honestly, Felicity was proud of herself, too.

"It's a surprise," Jackson said.

"One that requires a puffy coat and gloves?" she asked, looking down at her arms. He'd supplied the coat and gloves and had even offered a knit cap, but she'd stuffed that in her pocket in case she needed it later.

"We're outside at night, right?" he said as he rounded the storage building and waved at the snowmobile that was sitting there with the key in the ignition.

"We're going on a snowmobile ride? Now?" she asked. Just as she said the words, the orchard behind her lit up with what seemed like a million twinkle lights. "Silent Night" started to play, and a very light dusting of snow started to fall.

"Looks like now is the time," he said, waving at the snowmobile. "You first."

"Oh my gosh. This has the fairies' fingerprints all over it." As she climbed onto the machine, she glanced back at him. "How did you get them to do this?"

"It wasn't me," he said as he stepped up behind her and took a seat. "I'm just the messenger."

"Oh, wow," she said softly, hardly able to believe that the fairies were putting on this show just for her. She'd worked at the orchard her entire life, and never once had they done something like that for her.

The only time they'd shown themselves to her was when her grandmother had passed. They'd been there singing a soulful song the day they'd said goodbye and scattered Kitty's ashes. Felicity also believed that they'd come to her in a dream, asking her to take care of the land as her grandmother had, but she hadn't been sure if that had been real or just her imagination working overtime.

An orb of light appeared in front of Felicity and then started moving toward the orchard. She knew without anyone telling her that she was supposed to follow it. With zero hesitation, she fired up the snowmobile and eased it forward through the trees.

It wasn't long before they came to a small clearing that had a fireplace, a cozy couch, and a tree that was decorated with candy and popcorn. She heard laughter ring out, followed by a shriek of delight right before a little blond girl came running into the meadow, stopping only when she got to the tree. An adult suddenly appeared and helped the little girl hang a homemade Christmas tree ornament that was made out of construction paper and candy.

Felicity sucked in a sharp breath. The little girl was her, and the adult was her grandmother. They'd spent the day doing crafts and making Christmas cookies.

Once the ornament was hung, Kitty swept up little Felicity and swung her around until Felicity was dizzy with joy. The scene vanished and was replaced by the image of the cabin and the tree that she and Jackson had decorated the night they'd been snowed in.

The orb moved on, taking them to a treehouse that was perched in one of the few maple trees that were on the property. The treehouse had been built by her father when she was very young, but never maintained, so now it was only a shell of what it used to be. But tonight the fairies had made it look like a gingerbread house with lights strung around the trunk. The snow fairies fluttered around it, showing her the scene of when her father had first shown her the little house. He'd helped her climb up into the structure, and then he'd read a favorite book to her. All she remembered was lying next to him with her head in his lap while he ran his fingers through her hair, reading *The Velveteen Rabbit*. It was one of the only cherished memories she had of her father before he'd left.

The memory made her chest ache, and she was happy when the orb moved on.

This time it stopped at the edge of a stream, showing a fluffy white puppy in the bright sun, playing in the water.

"Bixly!" she cried, and the dog she'd had as a kid ran over, jumping into her arms, giving her a sloppy kiss before he faded away. "Oh my gosh," she said, pressing her hand to her face where she could still feel the wetness from his tongue. "He was the best."

Jackson tightened his grip on her waist and leaned in as they moved on.

The final stop was another clearing, only it wasn't one she recognized. There were sweet little cabins that were all decorated for Christmas, a large tree in the middle, and fairy lights everywhere. The air was scented with something that smelled like peppermint and chocolate. If she hadn't known better, she'd have thought maybe they'd stumbled on a village at the North Pole.

But when ethereal fairies started to appear on the porches of the cabins, she suddenly understood. This was where the woodland fairies of the Hill property lived while watching over the land.

A red-headed fairy with long, wavy locks slipped into the clearing. She was wearing a green velvet dress with golden ties around the waist and had golden dangling balls for earrings. The necklace around her neck glittered like Christmas lights, and she was so beautiful she left Felicity momentarily speechless.

"Hello, Felicity," the woman said, her voice tinkling like delicate bells. "It's wonderful to finally meet you." She nodded toward Jackson. "It's lovely to see you again, Mr. Bell. Thank you for watching over Felicity for us."

"It's been entirely my honor," Jackson said.

Felicity whipped her head around. "You've met this fairy before?"

"She's the Christmas fairy," he whispered to her. "She asked me to help you find your Christmas cheer."

"You did all those things because a fairy asked you to?" she asked, feeling strange, like she'd been lied to or betrayed.

"No, I did them because I wanted to," he said. "Just like I am right now. I care about you, Felicity. And if that means helping the fairies that watch over you, then I'll do it every time."

She could hardly argue with that. Instead, she turned to the fairy in front of her. "Why did you ask Jackson to bring me out here?"

"To remind you why you love this property. So you can see it's worth fighting for."

Felicity scoffed. "I didn't need that reminder. It's ingrained in my DNA to fight for this land. I'm doing everything I can to make sure it doesn't end up in the hands of some opportunist who just wants it to build condos or tract homes."

"We know. That's why we want to help." The Christmas fairy waved a hand, making the tree disappear. In its place, a gorgeous trunk appeared. The top magically opened, and inside sat an intricately carved treasure chest. One Felicity had seen before.

But as soon as she registered what she was looking at, the box vanished just like the tree. This time all that remained was an old-fashioned key.

"That's for you, Felicity. Find the treasure chest, and you'll find what you need to keep this land safe," the Christmas fairy said.

"But I don't—" She abruptly stopped talking as an image of the chest on a fireplace mantel flashed in her mind. A mantel that she hadn't seen since the last day she'd seen her father. She swallowed hard. "I remember now."

The Christmas fairy nodded once and then slowly drifted off back into the trees. As soon as she disappeared, so did the other fairies and their charming houses, leaving Felicity and Jackson alone in the snow-covered woods.

The only thing that remained was the golden key that glinted in the snow.

Jackson climbed off the snowmobile, walked to the

center of the clearing, and retrieved the key for her. It was hot in his bare hand, almost too hot to touch. By the time he made it back to the snowmobile, his hand was burning from the heat.

"It's really hot," he said as she picked it up and tucked it into her palm.

"No it isn't," she said, staring at him with confusion as she held it up. "It's neither hot nor cold."

Jackson touched the top of the key one more time before snatching his hand away. "It feels like it's on fire to me."

She eyed it curiously and then nodded slowly. "It's meant for me and only me. I bet if I anyone else touched it they'd say it was too hot, too. But me?" She pressed the key to her cheek. It was hot enough to him that Jackson expected the metal to leave a mark. But when she pulled it away, there weren't any marks or imperfections, just her perfect, peaches-and-cream complexion. Felicity tucked the key into her pocket and said, "Ready?"

He tightened his hold around her and said, "Always."

CHAPTER 20

*J*ackson woke to the smell of fresh coffee and pancakes. He rolled over in the bed, reached for Felicity, but unsurprisingly, he came up empty. The fairies weren't the ones making the coffee.

With a groan, he rolled out of bed, pulled on his pajama pants and the fluffy robe, and then stuffed his feet into his slippers before he shuffled out into the cabin. The chill in the air had him pulling the robe tighter around him as he made his way into the kitchen.

Felicity was standing at the stove, spatula in hand, flipping a pancake. She glanced over at him and smiled. "Good morning."

Her hair was mussed, and she had a rosy glow that made him want to tug her back into the bedroom. But the scent of the pancakes hit him and made his stomach growl with anticipation. The hunger won out, but that didn't stop him from walking up behind her and dropping soft kisses on her neck.

Felicity shivered slightly, but he knew it wasn't from the cold. He'd already learned that she loved it when he kissed her there. She let out a contented sigh, leaning back against him. But when his hand slipped between the folds of her robe, she said, "Nope. We have things to do today."

Jackson let out a disappointed sigh and took a step back.

"Coffee's made," she said, pointing at the pot.

He poured himself a cup and then refilled hers.

"Thank you," she said.

"I'm the one who should be thanking you. Waking up to fresh coffee and breakfast? There isn't anything better than that."

She snorted. "We both know that's a lie, but there's no time for another romp in the bed, so this is second best."

He laughed and got the plates out of the cabinet. A few minutes later, they were both at the table eating the fluffiest pancakes that Jackson had ever tasted. "These are delicious. How do you get them so fluffy?"

"Thanks," she said. "The secret is to beat the egg whites and then fold them into the batter. That and buttermilk. My grandmother taught me."

He raised his coffee mug in a salute to Kitty Hill.

Felicity laughed and did the same.

Once breakfast was finished, Jackson waved her off. "I've got the dishes. Don't you need to get cleaned up and open the store?"

"Yes," she said with a sigh. "But I'd rather stay here with you."

He wrapped an arm around her waist and tugged her in close. His entire body came alive when her skin touched his, but all he did was lean in and give her a long lingering kiss. He had the night off, and they had a road trip they needed to take as soon as Felicity finished restocking the Holiday Cheer at her store. "Go on," he whispered. "Tonight we'll make up for what we missed this morning."

"Is that a promise?" she asked.

"You can count on it." He kissed her cheek one more time before turning his attention to the dishes. He could hear her in the other room getting ready for work, and Jackson knew that this was what he wanted from now until forever.

He wanted to wake up and spend his mornings with Felicity. He wanted to hear her getting ready for work. Do the dishes after they'd eaten breakfast. Spend his entire day off running errands with her. After years of dating women who always wanted to try to push him back into the corporate life, he'd finally found someone who accepted him on his own terms. He wasn't interested in climbing the corporate ladder. All he'd wanted to do was spend his nights cooking for the people at Sleighed and spend the rest of it hiking and skiing his favorite mountain. But now, he also wanted warm nights by the fire with the gorgeous blonde who always kept him on his toes. He wanted to wake up with her in his arms, eat her pancakes, and help her cut down trees that blocked her roads.

He wanted it all… with her. All he had to do was convince her that she wanted the same thing. But he wasn't at all sure he could.

After he finished the dishes, Jackson walked into the bedroom to find Felicity dressed and ready to go. She walked up to him, wrapped her arms around his waist, and kissed him lightly. He leaned into her, demanding more, and when her lips parted, he knew he'd won. Burying his hands in her hair, he showed her exactly how much he wanted her. How much he needed her, and only let go when her phone buzzed.

"Oops," she said. "That's Marilyn wondering where I am." She grinned up at him. "If I told her I was getting ready to rip your robe off, do you think she'd care if I'm late?"

Jackson wanted nothing more than that, but they had more important things on their to-do list that day. "I'm sure she'd forgive you, but the longer we linger here, the later it'll be when we get to Tahoe."

She frowned. "Yeah, I know. I guess it's time to be responsible."

He gave her one last kiss and then watched her go. Jackson headed for the shower and then spent the morning cleaning up the cabin until he heard the roar of a couple of vehicles outside. When he peeked out the window, he spotted two white vans and the silver Escalade. A couple of film crews spilled out of the vans. Larry jumped out of the passenger seat of the Escalade, but the driver didn't move. Jackson could tell by the silhouette that the driver was none other than Trace Rhodes.

Wanting to keep an eye on the man, Jackson slipped out of the cabin and quietly took a seat in the corner of the porch. It wasn't long before Trace pushed the door of the large SUV open and climbed out. The phone was still pressed to his ear as he started to pace.

Larry and the film crews had disappeared into the orchard, leaving just Trace and Jackson at the cabin, though Jackson was fairly sure that the other man hadn't even noticed him. He hadn't once looked his way, and he was talking loud enough that Jackson could hear almost every word.

"Listen, Vincent, I'm telling you that this is the next development opportunity. Did you get the pictures I sent? We can clear out the apple trees and plant a new vineyard."

Jackson frowned. Wasn't Vincent the name of Ernie's business manager? Was Trace actually talking to Ernie's nephew about Felicity's property? He leaned forward, straining to hear the rest of the conversation.

"Or we can leave the orchard and start a hard cider business. There's still plenty of acreage to plant grapes on the north side of the property. All we'd need to do is tear down that old store, add a tasting room and maybe a place for a four-star restaurant, and the money will be rolling in."

Jackson's blood started to boil. This jackass was definitely making plans for Apples and Spice and Everything Nice. Little did he know that if he tried to do any of that, Jackson would find a way to take him down. And if for some reason he failed, there was no way the fairies were going to tolerate him. If Jackson thought Trace had even a chance of taking over the orchard, he'd almost feel sorry for the poor bastard.

Trace started to walk toward the orchard, and Jackson followed, keeping a fair distance back so that the other man wouldn't notice him. But he was still close enough that he could hear Trace's side of the conversation.

"I'm telling you, cuz, once the foreclosure goes through and you find a way to transfer the property from your uncle, we can finally start our own empire. Along with the wine and cider, there are other opportunities, like adding more short-term rentals. Maybe a bed and breakfast or an inn and spa. There's already one cabin that's in pretty good shape. We could add more and really ramp up the cash flow."

Cuz? Cousin? Was Trace related to Vincent? Jackson made a note in his phone to check for any connections.

They made their way into the orchard and found Larry and the film crew. Larry was busy directing the crew to take scenery shots, and when the snow started to fall again, he got really excited and started shouting commands, telling them to get shots of everything.

Trace was still on the phone, only now he was listing all the ways he planned to use his imminent windfall and was talking about clear-cutting part of the land.

Magic sprang up out of nowhere, nearly knocking Jackson off his feet. Intense anger wrapped around him, pressing against his psyche before it morphed into the physical form of a swarm of angry bees.

Jackson watched in awe as the bees swarmed through the lightly falling snow, heading straight toward Trace.

The man's eyes went wide with fear just before he dropped his phone and took off at a dead run, heading straight for the film crew.

"Hey!" Larry shouted. "Trace, get the hell out of the shot. What are you doing?"

Trace screamed something about being allergic to bees as he grabbed one of the crew and held the man in front of him like some sort of shield. It made no difference, and the angry bees closed in, encircling them.

The crew member thrashed and threw Trace off, running for cover into a tent they'd set up to house their equipment. Trace was hot on his heels and barely managed to seal himself up in the tent before the bees caught up with him again.

Jackson studied the bees as they hovered near the tent, clearly waiting for their victim to reappear.

Trace screamed from inside the tent. "I need an EpiPen. Someone get my EpiPen!"

"I have one," one of the crew said as he fished it out of his messenger bag. He eyed the mass of bees warily and then handed the pen to someone else to deliver to the tent.

The bees buzzed angrily, and Jackson was convinced that the fairies would magically hold them there indefinitely until they found their prey. But then the snow started to fall at a faster rate, and the bees had trouble staying afloat as the wet snow pelted their small bodies.

Finally, Jackson felt the magic disappear as the swarm of

bees took off into the forest, no doubt looking for cover until they could safely make it back to their hives.

The fairies were gone, but the message was clear. If Trace managed to gain control of the land, they'd make his life a living hell every moment of every day. Jackson snickered to himself and started to head back toward the cabin.

But when he heard Larry start yelling, he stopped and turned to find the director in Trace's face, his finger raised as he chewed him out for ruining the shots.

"Now the lighting is all off and we'll have to reshoot. All because you couldn't keep out of the shot. How long have you worked for me? You know that filming is sacred!" Larry was screaming at him, his face getting redder by the second, and Jackson wondered if the man was on the verge of having a heart attack.

Trace had zero patience for the outburst though, and he met the director toe to toe. "I was being chased by bees, Larry. I could have *died*. Do you understand what that means, you self-important, egotistical jackass?!"

"How dare you speak to me that way. I could fire you on the spot," Larry sneered.

"You think that scares me?" Trace shot back. "Well how about this?" Trace raised both his middle fingers and said, "I quit!"

Everyone stood silent as they watched Trace stalk through the snow back toward the cabin.

"Good riddance!" Larry called. "Good luck getting back to town. That Escalade is rented to the film production!"

"I'll hitchhike if I have to," Trace called back.

"You won't work in this business again, you know that, right?" Larry shouted.

Trace ignored him, but Jackson heard him mumble something about starting his own business. Jackson hoped he wasn't referring to the orchard, because there was no way he was letting that man get his hooks into Felicity's land.

One way or another, Jackson would do whatever it took to make the foreclosure disappear, even if it meant paying the damned loan himself. He was too invested now. And no way was he letting the likes of Trace Rhodes take over *any* part of Christmas Grove.

CHAPTER 21

*F*elicity was busy packing up an order when Jackson walked in. She couldn't help the smile that broke out over her face when she saw him standing there, looking like he belonged on the cover of a magazine. He was far too handsome for his own good. "Hey," she said. "I'll be ready in just a few minutes."

"Take your time," he said as he turned to stare out the window.

Something was off. Jackson seemed tense, like he was on high alert, and she needed to know why. After she handed the package to her customer, she walked over to Jackson and said, "What are you doing?"

"Watching that jackass Trace Rhodes try to find a ride," he said, nodding at the man who was on his phone again and pacing around the parking lot.

"He's not staying for the filming?" she asked, curious about the drama.

"No, Larry fired him." Jackson turned to her. "But that's not even the craziest thing I heard this morning. I was on the porch and overheard Trace talking to someone named Vincent."

"As in Vincent Sinclair?" she asked, certain that couldn't be true.

"The one and only." Jackson gave her a brief rundown of how Trace was making plans for the orchard as if the man already owned it. "I don't know exactly what's going on, but it sounds like Trace and Vincent are planning on making sure the foreclosure goes through and then fleecing the property from Ernie."

"That's… crazy," she said, shaking her head. "You must have heard him wrong."

Jackson stared down at her and sadly shook his head. "I didn't. That man is planning something, and the fairies are not having it."

"Well, neither am I." Felicity didn't want to believe that someone was trying to steal her family land out from beneath her, but she trusted Jackson, and if he said he heard Trace making plans, then that was all she needed to know.

With her hands balled into fists, she strode out of the store and walked right up to Trace. "You need to leave my property right now."

He blinked at her and then gave her a look of extreme irritation. "I'll leave when I'm ready."

"No, Trace Rhodes. You'll leave right now." She pointed at the road. "You aren't welcome here. Get off my property, or I'll be forced to call the police and have you escorted off."

"What crawled up your butt?" he asked. "I'm not doing anything but waiting for a ride."

"*You* did, and I don't care what you're doing. Do it down at the road."

"The film company has a contract," he said. "You can't throw me off the property. You're being paid handsomely for our right to just stand around if we want to."

"That's where you're wrong," she said, crossing her arms over her chest. "It's come to my attention that you've been fired, which means that you no longer work for the film company that has a contractual right to be here." She gave him a sickeningly sweet smile and once again pointed to the road. "Go now, and just so we're clear, I never want to see your face around here again. Got it?"

Trace's face turned dark as anger flashed in his beady eyes. "Come January 1st, you won't have a choice. I'll be here with bells on, so enjoy your property while you can, Ms. Hill, but this time next year, you'll be the one who is not welcome here."

As he strode off, kicking up wet snow as he went, she called after him, "Over my dead body!"

He shrugged and called back, "That's a little dramatic, but it's your choice, I suppose. Good luck, Ms. Hill."

Felicity was so angry she was afraid she'd run after the man and throttle him.

"Are you okay?" Jackson asked as he placed a hand on her shoulder.

She suddenly became aware that she was so angry she was shaking, and she took several deep breaths, willing herself to calm down. Trace Rhodes would never have her property. Not even if she had to sell it to someone else to keep him from getting his grubby hands on it.

"Jackson, can you take me to Tahoe now?" She pulled the golden key that the fairies had left her the night before from her pocket and held it up. "It's time to find out what's in that treasure box."

"I'm ready when you are," he said.

"Let's go."

"I HAVEN'T BEEN HERE in years," Felicity said as she stood in front of the large home that sat back in the woods, hidden from the road. A Toyota 4Runner was in the driveway, the snow had been plowed, and there were boots sitting on the front porch. Add in the fact that soft light glowed from the front window, and there was every indication that someone was home.

"Did your parents share custody?" Jackson asked.

"No," she said, swallowing the bitterness that she always felt when she thought of how her father had just up and left for a new life. "My mom brought me to visit a few times, but every time we came, it was awkward and weird, and all I wanted to do was go home."

Jackson wrapped his arm around her shoulders. "I'm right here. Any time you want to leave, just give me the word."

She smiled up at him gratefully. "Thank you." Then she

took a deep breath, wondering if her father would even recognize her. Straightening her spine, she walked up to the door and knocked.

A dog started barking, announcing their presence, and then she heard it. Her father's voice.

"Quiet, Bruno. That's enough." The door swung open, and her father, who was holding a small white and gold dog, said, "Hi, can I help you?"

She stared at him. He looked pretty much the same. His hair was turning silver, he'd gained about twenty pounds, and there were lines around his eyes, but he was the same man she remembered. She cleared her throat. "Hello, Dad."

Surprise flashed over Gary Dillon's face before he lit up, his smile reaching his eyes. "Felicity? My goodness, you look wonderful."

His reaction took her off guard, and she gaped at him for a moment.

"Come in. It's cold outside." He opened the door wider and waved for her to enter his home.

"Um, yeah, okay." She led the way and heard Jackson introduce himself as he passed her father.

"It's nice to meet you, Jackson. Are you Felicity's partner?" Gary asked.

"No," she and Jackson said at the same time. Then Felicity said, "He's a friend. A good friend... though maybe more."

Jackson's lips twitched with amusement.

Gary chuckled and said, "I see." He led them deeper into the house until they were in his cozy living room and said,

"Take a seat. Do you want something to drink? I have water, tea, cocoa, soda. I'd offer a beer or wine, but there's no alcohol in the house."

"No," Felicity said, shaking her head as she and Jackson sat on the couch. "We're fine." It occurred to her that Jackson could have answered for himself, but her nerves had taken over, and she was having trouble processing everything. She hadn't expected her father to be pleased to see her. It went against everything she'd believed for the past twenty years.

Her father put the dog down on the floor, and the fluffy thing ran over to her, putting his paws on her leg as he begged for attention.

"Hey there, cutie pie. You're really sweet, aren't you?" she said to the dog, knowing that she was procrastinating.

Gary sat back in his chair, watching her. Waiting.

Finally, Felicity looked up at him, intending to ask about the treasure chest, but instead she blurted, "Why did you leave?" She clamped a hand over her mouth and shook her head. "Sorry, I didn't mean to say that."

"But it's what you needed to say," Gary said as he leaned forward and clasped his hands together. "There is no magic answer, Felicity. Nothing that can excuse my absence or explain why. I'm afraid the only answer is that your mother and I were toxic when we were together. She didn't want me around, and eventually, I just couldn't stay. It wasn't healthy for anyone."

Felicity studied him, hating that his answer seemed rehearsed, as if he'd spent a long time thinking about what he'd say when she finally came looking for him. "What's the real answer, Gary?"

His carefully cheerful expression vanished, replaced by a mix of pain and embarrassment. "You're a lot like her, you know."

"I'm more like my grandmother," she said with a sniff.

Gary cracked a hint of a smile. "That's true. You are." Then he stared down at his feet before he finally looked up and said, "The truth is that I was drinking too much, and your mother thought I was an alcoholic."

"Were you?" she asked.

He nodded. "Yes. I'm in recovery now."

"That's good. How long?" What she really wanted to know was why he hadn't contacted her once he'd gotten sober.

"Ten years." He picked up the dog that had run back to him and gave the creature his full attention, no doubt needing something else to focus on other than his only daughter.

"Why didn't you contact me?" she asked.

His head jerked up, and he locked eyes with her when he said, "I did. Many times."

"No, you didn't." She spat the words out, hating that he was lying.

"Felicity," he said softly, "I promise that I did. I wrote letters, hoping that someday you'd want to see me again." He got up from the chair, walked over to the mantel, and grabbed a wooden box. He set it on the coffee table, and Felicity let out a small gasp.

"It's the treasure chest," she whispered. "You still have it."

He frowned. "Of course I do. It belonged to your grandmother. I'm not sure how it ended up in my things when I left, but I always intended to send it back to her, and then…" He trailed off and shook his head as if he was trying to forget he'd said anything.

"And then what?" she demanded, needing to know what this box meant to him.

Sadness flashed in his green eyes as he said, "I suppose it felt like a lifeline to you. As long as I had that box, I thought that maybe it meant that we'd find a way back to each other. I know that's ridiculous, but—"

Felicity held up a hand, stopping him. "It's not ridiculous." Then she let out a bark of laughter as she pulled the key out of her pocket. "That box is why we're here."

He frowned, looking hurt. "You're not here to see me?"

She grimaced and started to shake her head, but then she stopped and said, "I'm here for the box, but maybe this is the universe's way of helping us reconnect."

A slow smile spread across his face. "Yeah, I guess so." Then he sucked in a sharp breath and opened the lid of the box, revealing a stack of letters. He handed her the one on top.

She scanned the address and nearly cried when she saw that it was addressed to her. But right there in her grandmother's handwriting were the words *Return to Sender.* She let out a small cry of frustration before she waved the letter in the air and asked, "Why would she do this?"

"I'm sure she thought she was protecting you," Gary said.

"When I called and asked her about it, she said that you were finally in a good place after losing both your parents, and she didn't want anything or anyone upsetting you. She said to wait until you started asking about me, then she'd facilitate a meeting. But that call never came, and although I still sent letters, they always came back. Eventually, I stopped and just saved them all for the day you finally came to find me."

Felicity sat back on the couch, trying and failing to process what she'd heard. How could it be true that her grandmother had kept her father from her? But had she? Really? Felicity had always known where he lived. Kitty had even asked her periodically if she wanted to try to reconnect with him, but she'd always been adamant that she didn't. Kitty was the only one she needed.

Her grandmother had respected her choices, telling her it was her decision but that it was always okay to change her mind.

But why hadn't Kitty told her about the letters? Would that have changed things?

Felicity didn't know. After her mother died, she'd had a rough time, and to this day if she was honest with herself, she knew she had abandonment issues. It's why she'd always been adamant that she didn't want to get married. She'd been just as adamant about not wanting to reconnect with her father.

She didn't know what her grandmother was thinking, but one thing was for sure; Felicity was determined not to resent the one person who'd always been there for her no matter what. She assumed that Kitty did what she thought was best for her granddaughter, and that was that.

Felicity stared at the treasure box and frowned. "You didn't need the key to open the box."

"What?" Gary asked.

"This key is supposed to help me find something important," she said, feeling deflated. Had the fairies gotten it wrong? Was there another box she was supposed to find? Her heart sank. She'd thought she was close to finding something that would help her clear up the lien on the property, but it appeared that the fairies just wanted her to reconnect with her father. Did he know something about the loan?

She looked up, about to ask Gary if he knew anything about it, when he picked up the box and turned it around, showing her a secret locked compartment.

"Does the key fit here?" he asked.

Felicity jumped to her feet, slid the key into the lock, heard it click, and then let out a squeal of excitement when the compartment opened, revealing a slip of paper. She grabbed it and held it up so that both she and Jackson could read it. She started to scan the text but barely got a quarter of the way through it before Jackson clutched her arm.

"That's it," he said. "That's the proof you've been looking for."

"Where?" she asked, still scanning the paper. "Show me where it says that loan was paid in full."

He pointed to a stamp on the side. "It's faded, but it has a date, a paid in full mark, and there is a raised notary stamp.

Run your fingers over it right here." He pointed to the bottom of the page.

She touched the stamp and then looked up at him with tears in her eyes. "This will hold up in court, right?"

"Absolutely." He grinned at her. "The fairies did more than one thing right today."

She laughed. "They sure did."

"Does someone want to fill me in on what's going on?" Gary asked.

Felicity held the paper up. "Did you know about a loan that grandma Kitty took out against the orchard?"

"Loan? No. I can't even imagine her doing that," he said.

"I couldn't either, but it appears she did a long time ago, and the loan came due this December. I was served with foreclosure paperwork, and since I had no knowledge of any loan, you can imagine how confusing that was." She waved the paper, still giddy at their find. "This right here proves that she paid it off, and all I need to do is file it with the county to get the lien voided."

"Wow. And it was here the entire time?" Gary glanced at the box.

"It appears so." Felicity clutched Jackson's arm and said, "We should get back before it gets too late."

He nodded and then looked at Gary before glancing back at her. "Need a few minutes? I can wait in the car."

"Yes, please," she said.

Gary picked up the chest and handed it to Jackson. "Felicity should take this. It's hers now."

Felicity eyed the letters one more time and felt a pang of

regret for all the years they'd lost. She knew that their relationship going forward wasn't going to be easy, but she did send up a silent thank you to the fairies for giving her the opportunity to try to repair what had been shattered years ago.

"Can I give you a hug?" Gary asked.

Felicity blinked back tears as she nodded.

For the first time in twenty years, Felicity's dad wrapped his arms around her and gave her a bear hug. She clung to him, holding on for a long time. Both of them were trying to make up for all the time that had passed. No matter how long they stood there, it would never be enough.

But it was a start, and that was what they both needed.

CHAPTER 22

"What do you mean I need the lienholder to sign off on it?" Felicity demanded as she stared at Doris. They were back at the assessor's office the next morning, trying to get the lien against her orchard removed so that the Sinclair Group would no longer have any claim to her property.

Jackson clutched her hand, trying to reassure her that everything was going to be fine. They had the necessary paperwork, and the rest he could work out. "Surely this is enough to prove that the lien is void," he said.

Doris nodded. "It definitely is. No doubt about it," she said. "Unfortunately, foreclosure paperwork has already been filed with the county. In order to get that dismissed so that Ms. Hill doesn't have to show up in court, she needs the other party to drop the claim. Or she can wait until the court date."

"When will that be?" Felicity asked.

Doris checked her ancient computer. "Looks like the end of January. If I were you, I'd do everything you can to get that signature. Once these things get tied up in court, things can get messy. I once saw a developer start bulldozing the day after the foreclosure date even though they knew their claim was bogus. They were able to say they had no idea, and then the owner of the property ended up selling to them at a discount because of the damage."

Felicity sucked in a sharp breath. "That sounds like grounds for a major lawsuit."

"It sure it," she agreed. "But who has the money for that? I just wouldn't risk it."

Jackson said, "Thanks, Doris. We'll get it taken care of." Then he placed his hand on the small of Felicity's back and guided her out of the office. The bright morning sun made him squint, and he had to shield his eyes just to lead her back to his truck.

"They wouldn't really start bulldozing things, would they?" Felicity asked, her voice strained.

"After that phone call of Trace's that I overheard, I wouldn't put anything past those bozos," Jackson said. "Let's just go to the Sinclair offices and get this taken care of today." The truth was, he was just as anxious to get the foreclosure paperwork settled as she was. During his years in business, he'd seen more than his fair share of shady business maneuvers, and Trace was just the sort of guy to try anything to get what he wanted.

"Yeah, okay," she said as she climbed into his truck.

Thirty minutes later, they were standing in the lobby of the Sinclair Group offices being iced out.

"I'm sorry, Ms. Hill, but Mr. Sinclair isn't available. I can leave a message," the receptionist said.

"Does leave a message really mean you'll throw all correspondence into the trash?" Felicity asked, her patience long gone.

"No, ma'am." The receptionist gave them a bored stare. "That's not what it means at all. Mr. Sinclair is a very busy man. You can't expect him to deal with every minor detail on everyone else's time frame."

"Well, Trina," Felicity said after reading the nameplate on the desk. "This isn't a trivial matter. It involves settling some paperwork on a property that your boss is trying to steal from me."

Her expression hardened. "There is no need to raise your voice. I am not your enemy."

"But you are defending the front line," she shot back. Then before Jackson knew what was happening, Felicity bolted for the office door that was just behind Trina.

"Ms. Hill! You can't go in there!" She quickly made a call, and as Felicity was rattling the doorknob, two security guards arrived and forcefully started to remove her from the building.

Jackson ran over to them. "You don't need to manhandle her," he said. "Let her go, and we'll leave."

"Sir, it's too late for that," one of the guards said. He grabbed Felicity by both arms and started to drag her toward the glass doors.

"Let me go!" she cried out.

The guard ignored her.

Jackson let out a growl of frustration and then strode up to the guard and grabbed his hands, trying to pry them from Felicity's arms. Unfortunately, the other guard pounced, and suddenly they were both being escorted out.

Once they were out on the sidewalk, both guards pushed them, and Felicity and Jackson both ended up laid out on the pavement.

Jackson looked over at her. "You didn't break anything did you?"

"No, but if that guard or receptionist gets in my way, I might break a finger or two."

He couldn't help it. He laughed. There were no circumstances in which he could imagine her hurting someone, but he had to admit that he was angry enough to consider it himself. He climbed to his feet, held a hand out to her, and then hauled her up.

She stared at the office building. "Should we stake out the place and wait for the weasel? I can bend his fingers back while you waterboard him until he signs off on the paperwork."

Jackson snorted. "As fun as that sounds, why don't we make a trip to see Ernie. Something tells me we might have more luck there."

"Okay, but I think waterboarding an old man might be taking things a little too far," she said.

"Come on, GI Jane," he said, shaking his head. "Let's get out of here."

"Fine," she said. But then looked back at the office building and added, "They're lucky I'm not the hexing kind. It's times like these when I wish I could curse them with ass boils."

"I wish you could do that, too," he said with a chuckle and then led her back to his truck.

BY THE TIME they pulled up to Ernie's house, Felicity had finally calmed down. Instead of talking about hexes, she was staring out the window wondering if a PR campaign would help her cause. "If I called up someone at the Christmas Grove Chronicle, I bet they'd print my story."

"They probably would," he agreed. Especially since the most they ever had to write about was who made the best gingerbread cookies for the annual Christmas fundraiser.

"If Ernie can't help, that's what I'm going to do," she said.

Jackson exited the truck and came around to open her door for her.

She smiled gratefully at him, and then together they made their way to Ernie's door.

Before they even knocked, the door opened and Ernie was standing there, grinning at them. "I knew you'd be back."

Jackson raised his eyebrows. "You did?"

"Sure. Young people always want to know about the past. And that's the one thing I have to offer." He gave his attention to Felicity. "You want to know more about your grandmother, don't you?"

"No," she said automatically. "I mean, yes, I will always want to hear stories about her, but that's not why we're here."

Ernie frowned. "Is this about that loan again? I already told you that my business manager will handle that."

"You mean Vincent Sinclair?" Felicity said with a snarl. "I'm sorry, Mr. Sinclair, but your nephew has no interest in dealing with me. I don't know if you directed him to ignore me or if he decided to do that all on his own, but here's where we're at. Not only won't he help me get the foreclosure case dismissed, but he and someone named Trace Rhodes are actively planning what they want to do with my property once they steal it from both of us."

"I think you'd better come in," Ernie said.

"I think you're right." Felicity held her head high as she followed the older man into the house.

Jackson felt himself smile with pride as he watched her come into her own. He had no doubt that no one had a chance against the feisty woman. She was a fighter, and goddess help anyone who came between her and something she loved.

Felicity glanced back at him. "Jackson, are you coming?"

He grinned at her. "I wouldn't miss this for the world."

Two hours later, Felicity, Jackson, and Ernie were at the courthouse filling out the paperwork to drop the foreclosure.

"Ernie Sinclair," Doris said, her eyes lighting with

pleasure as she walked toward them. "A little birdie told me you were here. How many years has it been?"

The older man leaned against the counter and flashed the assessor's clerk a brilliant smile. "Too many, Doris. Far too many. But I will say that time has been good to you. You don't look a day over forty."

"Oh, stop," she said, flushing from his praise. "Don't fib, Ernie. You know I'm forty-eight."

They both laughed and for the next fifteen minutes, Jackson watched Ernie flirt with the redhead until she finally said she needed to get back to her desk.

"Wait," Ernie said. "I hear there's a Christmas ball this Friday. If you're not otherwise engaged, I'd really appreciate it if you'd do me the honor of being my date."

Doris flushed from head to toe as she nodded with enthusiasm. "I'd love it."

"Great. It's a date." He winked at her, and as Doris hurried off, Ernie kept his gaze locked on her until she disappeared around a corner. Finally he looked at Jackson and Felicity. "I always did have a thing for redheads."

They both laughed.

Once they were done with the paperwork and Felicity had a copy of the canceled foreclosure, Ernie said, "Thank you for bringing this to my attention. Now I need to go fire my business manager. No one is allowed to try to cheat someone while using my name and resources. That's not how business is done."

"It's not?" Jackson challenged. "I read that you were pretty ruthless in your younger days."

Ernie gave Jackson a solemn nod. "Ruthless? Yes. A cheat? No. There's a difference." Then he walked off with his head held high.

"I like him," Felicity said.

"Me, too," Jackson agreed. Then he held his arm out to her. "Come on, badass. Let's go home."

"Home to the cabin?" she asked.

"Is there anywhere else you'd rather be?"

"Nope," she said, her eyes misting with emotion. "The cabin's absolutely perfect."

He cupped both of her cheeks with his hands and said, "That land won't ever be anyone's but yours. You believe that, right?"

One tear fell as she nodded. "I do. But maybe one day I'll have a daughter to leave it to."

"A daughter?" he asked, surprised. "Does this mean you might rethink maybe a husband, too?"

She shrugged. "Only if he's a good cook." Then she cackled and said, "One step at a time, Jackson. One step at a time."

"Just as long as you allow me to be around for each of them," he said.

She leaned into him as she grabbed his arm and said, "I think that can be arranged."

CHAPTER 23

"I look like a cupcake," Felicity said as she stared in the mirror.

Clara scoffed. "You look amazing. Your dress, your hair, your makeup. Jackson isn't going to be able to keep his hands off you."

"I'm not sure that's a good thing considering we're going to be in front of the entire town." Felicity didn't know why, but now that it was time for the Christmas ball, her nerves were out of control. She wasn't sure she should go at all. Wasn't it the type of thing that people went to when they loved Christmas? She didn't exactly fit that description.

But Jackson was taking her, and she really wanted to spend the evening dancing in his arms. *Dancing*. That was it. She'd just focus on that.

She glanced in the mirror and spotted the candy cane hair sticks holding her hair up and laughed. For someone who didn't like Christmas, she'd sure done her best to embrace it.

"You look amazing," Clara said again. "Who else could pull off that red and white number that looks like you've been gift wrapped?"

"It's too much, isn't it?" Felicity asked. The dress was red and white polka dots on the top and red and white stripes on the bottom. She'd added a red bow around her waist, showing off her slim figure. The candy cane hair sticks were just the icing on the cake.

"Nope. It's a Christmas ball. It's perfect." Clara went to grab her dress off the back of the door where she'd left it hanging and said, "I think I see Jackson's truck. Go on. I'll see you there."

"But I haven't seen your dress," Felicity said.

"You will." Clara shooed her out of the room. "Now go."

Felicity wondered what her friend was up to, but she did as she was told, and once she got outside, she stopped in her tracks.

Jackson was wearing a white suit with a red vest and tie, and she suddenly had a flash of stripping him out of it. She glanced back at the house she shared with Clara and wondered how much trouble she'd be in if she just dragged him inside and locked him in her room.

"Oh no, you don't," Jackson said, obviously reading her mind. "We're making an appearance at the ball. I promised the fairies."

She raised her eyebrows, wondering what that was all about but deciding not to ask. So far, the fairies hadn't steered her wrong. If they wanted her at the ball, then that was where she'd be. "All right. Let's go get our Christmas on then."

He held out his arm to her and when she clutched it with both hands, he said, "'I'm going to be the envy of the ball, having such a beautiful creature on my arm."

Felicity rolled her eyes, but couldn't help being tickled by his comment. Once they reached his truck, she glanced over at him and said, "You look a little too happy."

"Is that even a thing? Too happy?" he asked, amusement dancing in his eyes.

She shrugged. "I don't know. Maybe not, but you aren't even a little nervous, while I'm over here wondering what in the world I've gotten myself into."

He laughed. "Relax, Felicity. It's just a party. You like those."

"Sure," she said hesitantly. "But not Christmas parties."

He gave her a sympathetic smile. "Maybe this year it'll be different, and you'll be ready to embrace the magic that your grandmother loved so much. You could think of it as honoring her memory."

She didn't answer, but as she contemplated what he'd said, she thought maybe, just maybe, he might be right.

When they arrived at the square, Felicity kept waiting for the dread to kick in, but as they moved through the crowd, all she felt was excited anticipation. Everyone was dressed up, looking fabulous. Most had gone all out like she had, really making their outfits look like custom Christmas garments. And she wasn't the only one with candy hair adornments. Apparently, they were all the rage that year, and instead of making her embarrassed, she just felt like she was one of the cool kids who'd gotten the fashion memo.

They'd just grabbed a couple of glasses of champagne when Felicity heard shouting. "What in the world—" she started but then clamped her mouth shut when she spotted Jackson's mother, Eva, standing in front of Larry the director, screaming at him.

"You double-timing sack of garbage. How many people did you audition on your casting couch for this movie?" Eva demanded.

"Now, Evie, there's no need to get upset. I was just comforting Donna. It's not like—"

She threw her champagne right in his face, unwilling to wait for him to finish making excuses. "I want out of my contract with full pay," Eva said. "Make it happen, or you're looking at a sexual harassment complaint. Understand, Larry?"

"You'll never work in this town again," Larry snapped back.

"Fine by me since you're the main director here in this town. I wouldn't work for you again even if you were the last director on earth. I'd rather clean toilets than watch you run around acting like you're god's gift to women everywhere. I've got news for you, Larry. The only reason they ever gave you the time of day was because they wanted a part in your movie. But behind your back, they're all talking about the size of your peter." She held her pinkie finger up at half-mast. "It's not looking good for your reputation, my dear."

"Oh, Larry, there you are," Trace Rhodes said as he popped out of nowhere.

Felicity glared at the man, wondering if anyone would care if she punched him in the nose.

"Trace, what the hell do you want?" Larry snapped. "I thought you left town."

"I can't leave," Trace said. "Listen, Larry. I need my job back. I'll even take a pay cut, but you can't fire me. This is the job that is supposed to lead to better opportunities for me. I'm sorry about the other day at the orchard. I was—"

"Fine. Get a replacement actress for Eva's roll, and you can come back to work," Larry said.

"Are you serious?" Trace asked, looking a little stunned.

"Very. Just find me someone as pretty as Eva but who doesn't talk as much as her, and we're good."

Trace beamed at his boss. When he saw Felicity scowling at him, he quickly shuffled away, getting lost in the crowd.

"That was quite the show," Jackson said.

"Are you embarrassed that your mom was part of that?" she asked him.

Jackson laughed. "Hell, no. For the first time in forever, I'm proud of her. Good for her for telling that jerk off and growing a backbone. Maybe there's hope for our relationship yet."

"Do you mean that?" Eva said from behind them.

Felicity saw Jackson tense for just a moment before he turned around and said, "Sure, Eva. Just let me know next time you plan to visit. I'll make sure the guest room is ready."

His mom tackled him with a hug and then wiped her eyes when she let him go. "You're a good son, Jackson. Thank you."

He nodded at her and then said, "Nice dress. You look like a million bucks."

Eva beamed as she smoothed her red velvet dress.

Then an older actor appeared next to her and said, "Eva, do you want to dance?"

"Why, I'd love to, Eddie."

The pair walked onto the dance floor, gliding along like they'd been partners forever.

Jackson snorted. "That didn't last long."

"What didn't?" Felicity asked.

"Single life. I'll bet you ten bucks she's madly in love with Eddie by next week and will be planning to shack up in the new year."

Felicity shrugged. "At least she won't be at your house."

He laughed. "Good point."

Jackson held his arm out to her. "How about it? Gonna let me spin you around the dance floor?"

"I thought you'd never ask." She smiled to herself as he guided them into the crowd. And then when his arms went around her, she felt that distinct sense of Christmas wrap around her. The magic she hadn't felt since she was a kid. The scent of caramel apples combined with fudge and apple spice swirled around her, and she felt something let go in her chest. The ache that had been there since her grandmother had died lifted, and joy rushed into her heart.

Tears of happiness filled Felicity's eyes, and as Jackson twirled her around, she let them fall as if they were some sort of baptism that cleansed her of her pain and opened her heart again to everything she'd once loved. And to the man who held her in his arms and had somehow managed to help her unlock the magic of Christmas.

"Jackson," she said softly.

"Yeah?"

"Merry Christmas."

Jackson beamed at her and pulled her in close. Then right before he kissed her, he said, "Merry Christmas to you, too, gorgeous."

And in that instant she knew... One day she was going to marry Jackson Bell. But first she'd make him work for it.

CHAPTER 24

*C*lara Bowen sat in Sleighed on New Year's Eve, watching all her friends laugh and cuddle up with their partners. She, on the other hand, was sitting at the end barstool with only a warm beer for company. It was the same beer she'd been nursing for the past two hours. She just wasn't in the mood.

Just over eight days ago, the man she'd been seeing had up and left Christmas Grove without a word. She'd known it would happen. Hudson Snow was an actor. It was what they did. But that didn't mean she appreciated the ghosting. No one deserved that. Especially not after spending every day for three weeks with a person.

"Clara!" Danny called as he rushed over to her. "You need to dance."

"I don't," she said, shaking her head. The last time she'd danced, she'd been wearing a white formfitting dress that had shown off every curve and had made her date's eyes bug out. In fact, the dress had been so spectacular that she'd been nominated for the Christmas Queen at the Christmas ball. She'd been the first runner up. Clara would have been upset with the loss if the crown hadn't gone to Felicity.

Her friend had been so radiant that night that there was no denying she'd deserved the win. Felicity had even been a good sport about it, wearing the crown all night and proclaiming Christmas her favorite holiday again.

Clara didn't think her friend's new-found attitude about the holiday had anything to do with the contest—that honor went to Jackson Bell, who was currently glued to her side— but Clara had loved seeing the joy in her friend's eyes again.

"Come on," Danny said, tugging Clara off the stool and giving her a twirl. "Marissa is still serving drinks. Humor me."

Clara let out a tiny sigh, placed her warm beer back on the bar, and let Danny lead her around the dance floor for the next half hour. It was only when Marissa appeared to cut in that Danny actually let her go.

She knew that he'd been trying to cheer her up, and she'd appreciated it, but the truth was all she wanted to do was go home before the clock struck midnight. The very idea that she'd be the only one in the bar with no one to kiss… It was just too much.

Ten minutes before the countdown began, nobody was paying any attention to her, so Clara grabbed her coat and started to inch her way toward the exit. But just as she started to pull it open, a bubbly woman wearing a plum-colored dress cut her off.

Clara recognized her immediately. Her name was Sophie, and she was the sugar plum fairy who'd helped get Marissa and Danny back together after many years apart, and then she'd been the officiant at their wedding.

"Clara Bowen, where are you going?" Sophie asked.

"Home," Clara said, trying and failing to move around the fairy.

"I can't let you do that just yet," Sophie said, fluttering her translucent wings.

Clara let out a sigh. "Why? I'm tired, I don't have a date, and I don't particularly want to be here."

"Oh, but you do have a date. Sort of." She produced an envelope and handed it to her.

Clara read the script on the front of the envelope. It said *Open me at midnight.*

"What in the world—" Clara started to say, but before she could get the words out, Sophie vanished into thin air.

Her friends started to count down to midnight. "Ten. Nine. Eight..."

Jackson already had his arms around Felicity, and he was looking at her with heart eyes. But then when Clara studied Felicity, she was mirroring his sappy expression. Marrisa and Danny had stilled on the dance floor and were now swaying gently to the music. Every other couple in the place had gotten lost in the moment with their significant others, and Clara had a *letter.*

Perfect. It was exactly how she wanted to spend the evening.

Not.

"Three... two... one... Happy New Year!"

Confetti fell from the ceiling at the same time someone popped open a champagne bottle.

Clara ignored it all and ripped open the envelope. The air shifted, and Clara was no longer in the bar. She stood beside a lake, a horse next to her as Hudson Snow strode toward her, determination in his gaze when he said, "Clara Bowen, you're mine. Now and forever." And then he grabbed her and kissed her, making every muscle go weak with need.

Suddenly the air shifted again, and she was back in the bar, her lips tingling from the kiss as she wondered what in the world had just happened.

DEANNA'S BOOK LIST

<u>Witches of Keating Hollow:</u>
Soul of the Witch
Heart of the Witch
Spirit of the Witch
Dreams of the Witch
Courage of the Witch
Love of the Witch
Power of the Witch
Essence of the Witch
Muse of the Witch
Vision of the Witch
Waking of the Witch
Honor of the Witch
Promise of the Witch
Return of the Witch
Fortune of the Witch
Song of the Witch

Rise of the Witch
Charm of the Witch

Keating Hollow Happily Ever Afters:
Gift of the Witch
Wisdom of the Witch
Light of the Witch
Spell of the Witch

Witches of Befana Bay:
The Witch's Silver Lining
The Witch's Secret Love
The Witch's Lost Spell
The Witch's Hidden Garden

Witches of Christmas Grove:
A Witch For Mr. Holiday
A Witch For Mr. Christmas
A Witch For Mr. Winter
A Witch For Mr. Mistletoe
A Witch For Mr. Frost
A Witch For Mr. Garland
A Witch For Mr. Bell
A Witch For Mr. Snow

Premonition Pointe Novels:
Witching For Grace
Witching For Hope
Witching For Joy

Witching For Clarity
Witching For Moxie
Witching For Kismet

Miss Matched Midlife Dating Agency:
Star-crossed Witch
Honor-bound Witch
Outmatched Witch
Moonstruck Witch
Rainmaker Witch

Jade Calhoun Novels:
Haunted on Bourbon Street
Witches of Bourbon Street
Demons of Bourbon Street
Angels of Bourbon Street
Shadows of Bourbon Street
Incubus of Bourbon Street
Bewitched on Bourbon Street
Hexed on Bourbon Street
Dragons of Bourbon Street

Pyper Rayne Novels:
Spirits, Stilettos, and a Silver Bustier
Spirits, Rock Stars, and a Midnight Chocolate Bar
Spirits, Beignets, and a Bayou Biker Gang
Spirits, Diamonds, and a Drive-thru Daiquiri Stand
Spirits, Spells, and Wedding Bells

Ida May Chronicles:
Witched To Death
Witch, Please
Stop Your Witchin'

Crescent City Fae Novels:
Influential Magic
Irresistible Magic
Intoxicating Magic

Last Witch Standing:
Bewitched by Moonlight
Soulless at Sunset
Bloodlust By Midnight
Bitten At Daybreak

Witch Island Brides:
The Wolf's New Year Bride
The Vampire's Last Dance
The Warlock's Enchanted Kiss
The Shifter's First Bite

Destiny Novels:
Defining Destiny
Accepting Fate

Wolves of the Rising Sun:
Jace
Aiden

Luc
Craved
Silas
Darien
Wren

<u>Black Bear Outlaws:</u>
Cyrus
Chase
Cole

<u>Bayou Springs Alien Mail Order Brides:</u>
Zeke
Gunn
Echo

ABOUT THE AUTHOR

New York Times and USA Today bestselling author, Deanna Chase, is a native Californian, transplanted to the slower paced lifestyle of southeastern Louisiana and the Pacific Northwest. When she isn't writing, she is often goofing off with her husband, traveling, or playing with her two dogs. For more information and updates on newest releases visit her website at deannachase.com.

www.ingramcontent.com/pod-product-compliance
Lightning Source LLC
Chambersburg PA
CBHW020104180626
46812CB00006B/2461